"I'm never kind, Calvina, except for my own ends."

He touched her face with his free hand, caressing her cheek, then sliding his fingers into her free-flowing hair until they cupped her head. Deliberately he brushed his lips against hers.

"Your mouth is honey," he murmured. "How unwise of you to tempt me if you didn't mean it."

"Let me go," she whispered, hardly able to breathe.

"When I'm ready."

"You promised—"

"I consider myself freed from my promise."

He covered her mouth before she could answer. His lips were teasing but insistent, silently commanding her to yield her will to his. She fought to hold on to her true inner self, the only part left that seemed to still be her own. But the dark magic was at work again, making her lips soften and part for him.

By Penelope Stratton
Published by Fawcett Books:

THE UNROMANTIC LADY
THE DEVIL'S BRIDE

THE DEVIL'S BRIDE

Penelope Stratton

FAWCETT CREST • NEW YORK

A Fawcett Crest Book
Published by Ballantine Books
Copyright © 1997 by Penelope Stratton

All rights reserved under International and Pan-American Copyright Conventions. Published in the United States by Ballantine Books, a division of Random House, Inc., New York, and simultaneously in Canada by Random House of Canada Limited, Toronto.

Penelope Stratton has asserted her right to be identified as Author of this Work.

http://www.randomhouse.com

Library of Congress Catalog Card Number: 97-90245

ISBN 0-449-22597-6

Manufactured in the United States of America

First Edition: October 1997

10 9 8 7 6 5 4 3 2 1

Chapter One

"Careful, idiot! The water's too hot. You don't care how I suffer."

The voice of the selfish, ill-natured old woman rose in shrill complaint as it did every day. Calvina, kneeling by the basin on the floor, took a deep breath and controlled herself. Protesting would only make the tirade worse.

"I'm sorry for your suffering, ma'am," she said after a moment. "I mean only to make you more comfortable. I'll add a little cold water."

She tipped some into the basin in which Mrs. Dalrymple was soaking her feet. The old woman shrieked. "That's too cold. You want me to catch pneumonia."

"Indeed no—"

"Don't answer me back! *There!*" The old woman's hand struck Calvina a stinging blow across the face. She gasped and rose to her feet, her grayish-blue eyes blazing with anger, which she suppressed at once. Dearest, sainted Papa had taught her that anger was a sin, and she must turn the other cheek. But it was hard when nature had given her a spirited temper, and she was condemned to a life of drudgery with an old woman who delighted in humiliating her.

Having vented her spite, Sarah Dalrymple proceeded to indulge in a bout of hysterics. Her screams rose louder and louder, defying Calvina's efforts to placate her. At last the door opened and the large, shapeless form of Hugh Dalrymple appeared. Despite their differences of size and gender Hugh and his mother were uncannily alike, both having the same pinched mouths and small, mean eyes. He was dressed in the old-fashioned style, with a black, full-skirted coat and black knee breeches. This and his white neck bands made him look like a parson, which was his intention.

"Dearest Mama!" he cried. "What has happened? Tell me the worst at once."

"This stupid creature," Sarah shrieked. "She's torturing me."

"Ma'am, I protest—" Calvina started to say, but Hugh silenced her with an upraised hand.

"I do not believe that anyone addressed you," he declared loftily. "My ears may have deceived me, but I would be ready to swear that nobody in this room required you to speak."

Calvina fell silent.

"She's a clumsy idiot," Sarah declared vindictively.

"Indeed she is, Mama," her son soothed her. "We must regard her as a lost sheep, given into our care that we may guide and correct her. Are we not enjoined to practice forgiveness?"

"I'll forgive her if she will own her fault," Sarah said maliciously.

"Of course she will," Hugh said. "She is penitent, I'm sure." He looked inquiringly at Calvina.

"I'm sorry if I was clumsy, ma'am," she said with an effort. "I didn't mean to burn or freeze you."

"Liar!" Sarah said instantly. "You did it on purpose, you wicked thing, you. Confess!"

"Indeed, I cannot confess to what is not true," Calvina protested. "I was clumsy, no more."

"You dare to contradict me?" Sarah shrieked. She turned on her son. "You said she would be penitent."

"And so she is," Hugh said emphatically. "Come, no more of this, Calvina. It is not for you to dispute with your elders. Let me hear you own your fault."

2

"I have already admitted that I was careless," Calvina said. "I have no more to confess."

Hugh shielded his eyes with his hand. "She is proud and stubborn, oh Lord!"

"But I give you my word—"

"Forgive your wayward child, Lord!" Hugh bawled. "Let not her sin be writ against her—"

Calvina could endure no more. Slamming down the jug that she was still holding, she fled the room and ran upstairs to the tiny attic that was her bedroom. There she threw herself down on the narrow iron bed and pounded the pillow. Tears of anger and frustration poured down her cheeks.

"Oh, Papa!" she sobbed. *"Papa!"*

Only six months ago she'd had a position in the world as the daughter of Calvin Bracewell, parson and scholar. Although distantly related to an earl, her father was indifferent to worldly rank. He had a small parish in the university town of Oxford, and he had written many learned books. His reputation stood high. His books were studied in the colleges, and he was often invited to preach to the students.

With this he was content, being a simple man, who disliked luxuries and adornment, and who'd taught his daughter to scorn them also. But despite the austerity of his nature he was gentle and kindly, and he'd loved her. Calvina's mother had died when she was ten, and she'd become the little woman of the house, caring for her father and growing up close to him.

Then he had died, leaving her penniless. She'd been seeking a situation as a governess when Hugh Dalrymple, an acquaintance of her father, had offered her a home.

At first she'd been grateful, but after a few weeks at the Dalrymple home in Bath she knew she would have been better off as a governess. On the day she arrived one of the maids was dismissed. Thereafter Calvina was a drudge, bullied by Hugh and his wife, forced to care for

3

Hugh's spiteful mother, and tormented by Eglantine, his spoilt daughter.

A step on the stair made Calvina sit up hurriedly. She opened the door to Hugh and stood aside in silence for him to enter.

"I have come in grief, my child," he proclaimed. "It breaks my heart that one to whom I have offered the shelter of my roof should repay me with a stubborn, wilful temper, and even vent her spite on the white hairs of my ailing mother."

"It's untrue," Calvina said fiercely. "I am not spiteful. What happened was an accident."

"What happened was the work of the devil, manifesting himself through your pride. Oh yes, I know the haughty arrogance of your spirit. You seek to mask it beneath a meek air, but I see through you. You have grand relations. You think yourself superior to my family."

"But I never think of my 'grand relations.' It is you that talk of them all the time. . . ."

Hugh held up a hand to silence her. "You wound me deeply when you speak in that way, Calvina," he said. "It makes me feel that all I've done for you has been for nought. But I do not despair. I shall do my duty to you, to myself, to my cloth."

"What cloth?" Calvina demanded, stung. "You speak as though you were in holy orders."

Hugh took a sharp breath. It was true that he had never been ordained, but he dressed like a parson, and behaved, as he thought, in the manner of one. Most people accepted him vaguely as "something in the church," and deferred to him accordingly. But he couldn't delude Calvina, and the knowledge made him uneasy and spiteful in her presence.

" 'Tis not the outward attire that maketh the man of God," he intoned, "but the humble heart within. We will discourse no more on this head. It does not become you

4

to dispute with your elders and betters. Kneel, and we will pray for you to receive the grace of a penitent heart."

For an hour he tried to force her to admit that she'd treated Sarah with deliberate spite. Calvina resolutely refused to confess to something she hadn't done, although she was aching all over. In the end Hugh let her go because Sarah was shrieking for attention, which nobody else wanted to give. It was a victory of sorts, but one which left her heavyhearted, and for which she knew she would be made to pay later.

The journey from London to Bath normally took a whole day, but Lord Rupert Glennister did it in six hours, driving his curricle at a breakneck pace and frequently changing the black stallions he kept stabled on the road.

He'd left London in a rage that hadn't abated when he pounded up to the door of Glennister Court, his magnificent countryseat. Instantly grooms ran out to attend to the horses who were lathered from the journey. He leapt down, tossed the reins with a curt nod, and strode into the great hall.

"There you are at last, my dear boy!"

A plump, middle-aged woman with a smiling face came toward him, her arms outstretched in greeting. He gave her a vigorous hug and the hard expression in his dark eyes relaxed.

"You speak as though you knew I was coming," he said abruptly. "I told no one."

"News of your doings travels fast, and I have many friends in London. Come into the library. I have your favorite brandy waiting."

"So Lady Emsworth has been gossiping? Or is it Lady Curzon? There's always someone with time to chatter about what doesn't concern them."

"People have been talking about you ever since you were fifteen. You should be used to it by now," Aunt Josie said comfortably. "At one time you didn't mind being called the wickedest man in London. You rather enjoyed it."

"That was before it began interfering with my pleasures. It's the outside of enough when Lady Allbright tells me to my face that I'm not a fit person to meet her daughter when she makes her debut next month. Sally Allbright, who was glad enough to have me in her bed when that blockhead she married grew too much for her!"

This was very frank speaking for a lady's ears, but Aunt Josie had never been given to hysterics, and Lord Rupert had grown up saying exactly what he thought in front of her. Nor did she disappoint him now, for she said calmly, "Dear Sally! A nice girl but such a terrible hoyden. What her family would have done if they couldn't have married her off quickly, I dread to think. Is it true that you fathered her youngest boy?"

"How the devil should I know?" Rupert said impatiently. "Possibly. But I'm not the only candidate. That's what makes this latest start of hers so incredible, not to mention damned impertinent."

"I don't suppose you *want* to meet Julia Allbright," Aunt Josie observed. "You've always said that young girls fresh from the schoolroom were dead bores."

"They are. But that's not the issue. To be told that my 'sullied reputation' makes me unfit for decent females to meet is the outside of enough."

"The Allbrights are probably afraid she'll fall in love with you, the way all the other young girls seem to. They're hoping to marry her off to Walton."

Lord Rupert gave a snort of contempt. "The man's an idiot."

"But a very rich, titled idiot," Josie reminded him. "And on the lookout for a wife, which you most certainly are not."

"God forbid! The last thing I want is a legshackle, expecting me to act the family man and having the

6

vapors every time I'm away from home. That's what makes the suggestion all the more outrageous."

"What suggestion?"

"Sally Allbright had the effrontery to say that my position in society could only be recovered by marriage to a female of impeccable virtue."

"Nonsense, dear!" Josie said placidly. "No virtuous female would have you."

He scowled at that comment. Then his face broke into a smile that made it briefly delightful. "That's giving me my own again," he said appreciatively. "But the question doesn't arise since *I* would not have her. Virtuous females bore me. They're all bracket faced. That's why they're virtuous. Anyway, I don't know any. Never bothered to cultivate their acquaintance. Why should I?"

He poured himself another brandy and drained it. Josie judged it tactful to let the subject drop. She knew a good deal more than Rupert imagined, having received a stream of letters from her oldest friend Honoria, Countess of Maybury. Honoria was in her sixties, had been married three times, and was, by her own account, "an evil old woman." She lived at the heart of fashionable society and thrived on scandal.

She'd written recently:

Rupert seems intent on making London too hot to hold him. He's known as Devil Glennister, sometimes to his face, which only makes him laugh. Of course, I discount the more lurid tales of satanic practices, but people ask how his astonishing luck with the cards can be explained except by mysterious powers.

He fills his house with women of a kind that no decent female is supposed to know about (although, naturally, we all do). He recently had three spend the night and is reported to have worn them all out by morning. Maybury pretends to be shocked but, of course, he's wild with envy, and so are all the men. They say that only a pact with the devil could have made Rupert so *untiring*, but that's just jealousy.

The young girls are mad for him. That air of wickedness is a potent lure, and the fact that he ignores them simply makes them worse. It's a pity nature made him so desperately handsome. He's got away with doing and saying just what he likes for too long. It would do him good to want a woman who didn't want him. But I suppose that's asking for the moon.

Looking at her nephew now Aunt Josie understood what Honoria had meant about Rupert's looks. He was tall and loose limbed, with a slim body full of nervous energy. He'd been a beautiful child and then a startlingly good-looking boy. Now a man in his midthirties, he had lean features, and a sensual mouth that was too often curled in a smile of derision or contempt. The boyish beauty was gone. Instead there was the handsome, cynical face of a man who'd tried all that the world had to offer and no longer cared for any of it. His deeds had earned him the name "Devil Glennister," while his jet-black hair and dark eyes underlined it.

He laughed in the face of society's censure, even flaunting his reputation by driving black horses and sometimes wearing black apparel. But now, it seemed, society had struck back. He might be indifferent to social acceptance while it was his for the asking, but to be excluded was a stinging insult to his proud spirit. And it had maddened him.

All this Aunt Josie read clearly enough in Rupert's restless pacings and his black-browed expression. The haughty Glennister pride he'd inherited from his father made it intolerable to him to be judged, and to be judged by those he despised had driven his temper to a murderous pitch.

He stopped before her and his cynical features soft-

8

ened. "So you see, the black sheep has returned," he said. "Don't you have a scold for me?"

"Much heed you'd pay!" she retorted with spirit. "I remember you when you were a little boy in nankeen breeches, kicking up larks to get your father's eye. I left off scolding you then."

"What a wise woman you are!" he said, smiling and carrying her hand to his lips.

Aunt Josie was one of only two people in the world who had Rupert's affection. The other one was his cousin Ninian, a poor relation who lived at the Priory and managed the estates. He entered now, and a smile illuminated his gentle, serious face.

"By all that's wonderful!" he exclaimed, coming forward with his hand outstretched.

"You won't think it's wonderful when you hear my tale," Rupert said. "I've been setting the world by the ears." He spoke sardonically, but he clasped his cousin's hand with both his own, and his eyes were warm.

"I'll swear you said the same thing when you were expelled from Eton," Ninian responded. "Or was it Oxford?"

"Since I was sent down from them both it hardly matters," Rupert said with a shrug. "This time the ton has shut its doors in my face. I'm a libertine, a scandal, a disgrace to my name, and a great deal more, I daresay. Damned impertinence!"

"It's outrageous that they should treat you so," Ninian said warmly. "But sometimes, Rupert, I think you bring it on yourself out of sheer perversity."

Rupert shrugged. "They insist on seeing me as the devil. I oblige."

"But if they knew you as I do," Ninian persisted, "how decent and good you really are—" He stopped, for Rupert had held up his hand in horror.

"I beg you not to talk such fustian, my dear boy! If anyone were to hear you, think of the damage to my reputation."

9

Ninian gave a reluctant grin and subsided.

"Rupert can't show his face in society again until he's married a virtuous woman," Josie said.

"But that would be ideal!" Ninian exclaimed joyfully. "It's about time you—"

"Good God, man, you don't think I'm going to do any such thing, do you?" Rupert demanded, appalled. "Where are your wits? Join me for a drink in the library when I've changed my clothes."

"I will. There are a great many estate matters that need your urgent attention—"

"That's what I feared." Rupert abruptly left the room, taking the brandy with him. Ninian exchanged a rueful smile with Aunt Josie and followed him.

The Dalrymples lived in the second tier of Bath society, below the aristocracy but above the wealthy merchants. They had a carriage, a decent-sized house in Monmouth Place, and a modest but acceptable number of servants. Calvina's arrival had improved their standing. Hugh introduced her everywhere as "a cousin of Lord Stoneham," despite her protests that the connection was but distant.

This meant that he couldn't entirely treat her as a drudge. She was included in all invitations and must be allowed to accept, lest the invitations dry up.

Tonight they'd been invited to a little soiree given by Lady Jellineck. Both Hugh and his wife, Maria, disliked this woman, who patronized them.

"The widow of a paltry knight," he fumed as he regarded himself in his bedroom mirror.

"My love, you're taking all the room," the wife of his bosom complained, trying to see into the mirror.

He shifted an inch, and continued with his diatribe. "Born common Lucy Driver, husband in trade, got himself knighted by greasing palms, and then only because they had no sons to inherit the title."

10

"And the way she loads herself with rubies isn't to be borne," Maria added peevishly.

"You should have married a wool merchant, Maria," Hugh said sarcastically. "Then you'd have had all those baubles."

Years of marriage had taught his spouse the proper response, and she produced it now. "I preferred to marry a *gentleman*, Hughie. Blessed is she that seeketh not the things of this world but chooseth a godly husband."

"My love!"

"My love!"

They pecked at each other's sour lips.

"Anyway," Maria continued in a more prosaic tone, "Selwyn Jellineck was always a vulgarian." She'd been telling herself this for twenty years, since the day he'd offered for Lucy Driver and not for her.

"And his widow is worse," Hugh chimed in. "She queens it as though she'd never heard of trade. Mind you, she does give very good dinners." This was a sore point, as their own slatternly cook had spent the last two days in a drunken stupor.

When they had all crammed into the carriage there was some jostling for places, and Calvina ended up next to the window nobody else wanted because it let in a draft. Eglantine sat beside her.

"If only you'd buy a new carriage, Pa," Eglantine said fretfully as they rumbled to Great Pulteney Street. "This one is too small for five of us."

"What does the holy man need with new carriages?" Hugh rebuked her.

"This one was well enough before we opened our doors to Calvina," Maria snapped. "Ah, if only she were blessed with a grateful heart and would squeeze up a little."

"I'm squeezed up as tight as I can," Calvina protested.

"Ooh, you lying thing, you!" Eglantine exclaimed, giving her a vicious pinch. "You're taking up all the

11

room. Just because you've got fine jewels you give yourself airs."

"But I have no fine jewels—"

"That pearl looks very fine to me," Hugh said. "Too fine for a young woman in your circumstances."

Calvina instinctively laid her hand over the tiny pearl brooch that she wore. "It was my mother's," she said quietly.

"Pa, why can't I have pearls?" Eglantine whined. "They'd suit me much better than Calvina."

Almost anything would have suited Eglantine better than what she was wearing. Her white-muslin dress was so adorned with ribbons, bows, and flounces, that the effect of youthful innocence was marred. Moreover, white made her sallow complexion look like cheese. To make matters worse, her hair was curled in bunches over her ears, which broadened her already plump face.

Calvina was dressed in gray, her light brown hair done in demure braids, but beside Eglantine the beauty of her warm skin and delicate features glowed.

She glowed also for another reason. Tonight she would see Toby Aylesbury and know a few moments of happiness. Without Toby her life would have been bleak indeed. His mother was a crony of Lady Jellineck. His father had made a modest fortune in trade, most of which had gone to his elder brother.

Calvina loved Toby for his kindness, his gentle speech, and the way his eyes grew warm whenever he looked at her. She knew he loved her as much as she loved him and meant to offer for her formally, "when the time is right." This was a reference to his mother, who hoped to marry him to money. But she was a good-natured woman and could be won over at last. Then Calvina's wretched life would be ended, and her dream of happiness would begin.

Beneath her dress, carefully hidden, was the only other adornment she possessed. It was a small locket that Toby had bought her from a street vendor. It was valueless, except for the picture of himself that was hidden inside. The Dalrymples complained about her pearl, but they never guessed at the treasure she wore over her heart.

It was winter and the streets were pitch-dark at eight o'clock. All over Bath the citizens were venturing forth for an evening's pleasure. Lost in thoughts of Toby, Calvina saw nothing. But Eglantine peered past her out of the window, on the lookout for any excitement. At last a holdup in the road ahead forced the carriage to halt, and Eglantine gave a little excited scream.

"Look, Pa! We're in Barton Street. They say 'the Devil' lives here."

"I beg your pardon?" Hugh stared at his daughter.

"Lord Rupert Glennister. They call him 'the Devil' because he's so wicked."

"And pray what do you know of such people, miss?"

"Oh, *Pa*! Everyone knows about him. They say he's so steeped in infamy that ladies swoon when he appears. And when he gambles he gets the devil to blow on the cards so that he never loses."

"Daughter, I forbid you to look," her mother exclaimed. "If he should appear you might be turned to stone." As she spoke she was jostling her way across the carriage, the better to see.

"We must pray for this poor lost creature," Hugh asserted. "Let us be the instruments of his redemption."

But before he could begin the front door of a house was opened by a footman. It was on Calvina's side of the coach, and she had a clear view of the man who appeared. He was dressed for the evening in black-satin knee breeches, and a black coat of superfine, molded to his powerful shoulders. Even his hair was black, and in the shadows from the streetlamp it was easy to believe that this was a limb of Satan. Eglantine and her mother gasped in delighted horror, and Calvina regarded him curiously.

She'd never seen such a man, so tall, so broad of

shoulder, so well set up, such a handsome set to his head. Then she was horrified by her own thoughts. She was too levelheaded to believe Lord Rupert was the devil, but his sinfulness was legendary. His fine appearance was but a snare for the weak willed.

He glanced at the carriage, then made a small alert movement, as though something had arrested his attention. Time seemed to stop. His dark eyes gleamed and something went right through Calvina, making her heart beat faster. His gaze was fixed directly on her, and she felt as though a mysterious bond was linking her to this stranger, and it was growing tighter—and tighter—

A scream from Eglantine broke the spell. "Ma, he looked at me. The devil looked straight at me. Oh, I shall die, I know I shall."

Hugh began to pray madly. His mother set up a wailing, and Maria struggled for her smelling salts.

"Try to calm yourself, Eglantine," Calvina begged. "He can't harm you. He is only a man."

But Eglantine wasn't going to give up her moment of melodrama so tamely. "He's the devil," she moaned. "And he cursed me. But you care nothing for the feelings of others."

"I care very much for your feelings," Calvina protested. "That is why I would spare you alarm."

She took the smelling salts from Maria and tried to administer them, but Eglantine writhed, crying out in thrilling tones, "I am lost, I am lost," and swooned carefully into Calvina's arms.

Calvina tried to keep her thoughts charitable, but she knew Eglantine was thoroughly enjoying herself, and for a moment a touch of exasperation showed on her face.

Something made her look out of the window again. The man was still there, grinning. He'd seen and understood everything, she thought, and frowned to show him her disapproval. But he only laughed aloud, with complicity in his eyes, inviting her to share his amusement at

14

these ridiculous antics. Calvina turned away quickly, her face flaming with disturbing consciousness. He was a rogue, a man to be avoided and prayed for. Yet for a shattering instant she could almost have said, with Eglantine, "He has looked at me. I am lost."

In ten minutes they drew up in Great Pulteney Street. Toby appeared and assisted each of the ladies from the coach. He seemed to treat Calvina the same as the others, but she felt the warm pressure on her hand and saw the glowing look he gave her. It was over in an instant, but Eglantine noticed, and her eyes narrowed. The next moment she rearranged her face into a mask of girlish innocence and claimed Toby's attention.

There was much company tonight. Several of Lady Jellineck's elderly cronies had dragooned the junior members of their family into coming with them. Two young men were sulking at being forced to do the pretty, until they saw Calvina and their faces lit up.

She refused to respond, however, seating herself modestly close to the wall, while Eglantine flirted and giggled with the young men who were too gauche to escape her clutches.

Calvina received a benevolent smile from Mrs. Aylesbury and hope flared in her heart. Toby had been promising to speak definitively to his mother. She knew it was hard for his gentle nature to take a firm stand, but perhaps this graciousness meant that he had done so.

Among the guests who were new to Calvina was Mrs. Elphinstone, a woman of enormous self-consequence and no taste whatsoever. She was garishly dressed in a gown of puce satin, with a matching turban adorned with a huge feather, and a diamond brooch that needed cleaning. She viewed Calvina through her quizzing glass and remarked, "Calvina! Strange sort of name!"

"I was named after my father, ma'am. He was called Calvin after John Calvin of Geneva."

"Never heard of him," proclaimed Mrs. Elphinstone, as though that settled the matter.

"Never heard of John Calvin?" Hugh exclaimed as though personally affronted. "That sainted man whose austere life was a rebuke to those who indulged in luxury, whose—"

"I believe dinner is ready," Lady Jellineck interrupted him.

Hugh puffed and fumed, but the company was rising to follow their hostess into the dining room where a long table was set with china, crystal, and silver.

"Ladies, gentlemen," Lady Jellineck announced, "you see your dinner."

This way of proclaiming that there would be only one course found no favor with Hugh, who'd been hoping for a lavish repast. But Lady Jellineck's idea of one course was on a grand scale. The table groaned under game, beef, hash of mutton, chine of veal, and rabbit fricassee, rounded off with orange pudding, cherry tree in blanc mange, and mince pies. Best of all was a chocolate cream made by Lady Jellineck's peerless Antoine, and which Calvina liked so much that she felt guilty about dear Papa's strictures on mortifying the flesh. It was only by remembering that he'd permitted himself the occasional cigar that she could enjoy the second cream that Toby pressed on her.

After dinner there was music from the young ladies of the party, most of whom could sing or play to some degree. Eglantine was in her element, for although she didn't practice enough to play accurately, she performed, according to her mama, with great feeling. Since her voice could also carry a tune she passed as an accomplished young lady.

Calvina was at a disadvantage, never having learned to sing or play an instrument. But she wasn't much to be pitied, for Toby slipped into the seat beside her, and under cover of Eglantine's song, squeezed her hand.

"It seems so very long since I saw you," he murmured.

"I've hardly known how to bear it," she whispered back. "I've thought of nothing but you."

A more worldly-wise young woman would never have made such an admission. But Calvina had no wish to flirt and wouldn't have known how. Her nature was as honest, clear, and fresh as spring water.

"Your mother greeted me very kindly tonight," she said softly.

"I'm glad. I've been praising you to her, and she said that you were very prettily behaved."

"Does that mean she has consented to our engagement?"

"I—well, I haven't exactly put it to her as strongly as that. I'm persuading her by slow degrees. But she warms more to you every day, and when the moment is right—"

Calvina was silent. Toby knew best, and she must be content to leave matters to him. But if only he could steel himself to be firm.

The song ended. Under cover of the applause a footman entered the room and murmured something to Lady Jellineck.

"My dear," she said to Mrs. Aylesbury, "there is a visitor to see you. They went first to your home, then came on here, so it must be a matter of importance. Why don't you talk to them in the library?"

Toby and his mother rose at once and left the room. They were back in a few minutes, announcing their intention to depart at once. "My uncle George is ill," Mrs. Aylesbury said urgently. "He may not last the night."

Everyone expressed the proper concern, and within a few moments the Aylesburys were gone. No sooner had the door closed behind them than Lady Jellineck said comfortably, "I've ordered fresh tea and some more cakes."

"Dear ma'am," Hugh said, "your generosity is legendary. But let us first spare a moment for this poor

17

creature, about to meet his maker. Surely we should lift up our hearts, imploring help for his arduous journey—"

Before his hostess could protest he'd dropped to his knees, forcing everyone else to do the same, and keeping them there for ten minutes while his voice rose and fell dramatically. Calvina felt ashamed for him. Her father had many times uttered this kind of prayer, but he'd done so quietly, in humility of heart. The Reverend Bracewell would have died rather than put on this self-glorifying display.

She saw the door open and the footman ready with the tray. His eyes popped and he backed out hastily. Evidently Lady Jellineck saw this, too, for she rose from her knees and said bluntly, "That's enough of that. George Aylesbury has been at death's door many times these ten years. He always summons his family for the pleasure of tormenting them. Pray in your own time, not in my drawing room."

She rang the bell and the tea tray reappeared. Hugh fumed but was silent. To cover the awkward moment Calvina said, "His family must be very much attached to him, ma'am."

"Lord no, my dear, only to his money. He's got a tidy sum put away and he changes his will every year. It's like musical chairs. They all hope it'll be their name on the will when the music stops, if you see what I mean."

"An unfortunate attitude," Hugh declared loftily. "Ah, the lust for money! What havoc it can bring!"

Lady Jellineck gave a crack of laughter. "I should say twenty thousand pounds was worth a little havoc," she said coarsely.

It flashed across Calvina's mind that such a sum would make Toby independent and free to marry. Then she censured herself for worldly thoughts and looked quickly away, lest the others should detect her consciousness.

The party broke up early. After such a set down Hugh had no desire to linger, and he announced he would retire

18

early to spend some hours meditating on the Aylesburys and their tragic . . .

Here he caught Lady Jellineck's frosty eyes on him and hastily began to chivy his family out of the house.

Chapter Two

The silence in the gaming room was almost tangible. All other play had stopped so that everyone could watch the two men facing each other across the card table. One of them was sweating profusely. He was bloated with indulgence, his eyes bloodshot and desperate. Over the years he'd gambled away his own fortune, then his wife's. His children's inheritance had gone the same way. Lord Rupert already held his vowels worth ten thousand pounds. Tonight Fenton Bembridge had come in the wild hope of redeeming them, but instead he'd dropped another five thousand. But this time the luck *must* be with him. With a shaking hand Bembridge laid his cards on the table.

Lord Rupert shrugged and revealed his own cards. Four kings. A frisson went around the room, and Bembridge's face turned gray. "You've got to give me a chance to win it back," he said hoarsely.

Lord Rupert shrugged. "Is that wise? You won't win. Not this time, not the next, or the next."

"How can you be so damned sure?"

"It's enough that I'm sure. Haven't you heard that I never lose?"

"No man can win forever. You've got to play me again."

"If you insist. I'll stake the fifteen thousand you already owe me. What will you stake?"

"I have nothing left," Bembridge said savagely.

"You have a house in Henry Street."

"It—it's rightly my wife's property."

"That's never troubled you before. But no matter. If you'd rather not play . . ."

"Damn you! I have no choice."

"True. Give me your note for this last five thousand and we'll start again."

A boyish young man beside Rupert leaned down to murmur, "You can't do this. You'll put them onto the streets. He has three children."

Lord Rupert glanced briefly at the Honorable Charles Fitzcane, who'd accompanied him on this evening's round of pleasure. "You're a nice pup, Charles, but you interfere in what don't concern you."

"But—"

"I'll play this one to the end, as I play every game."

The young man's sensitive face twisted. "I thought the worst they said of you wasn't true."

"Always believe the worst. I've told you that often."

"I can't bear this. I'm going."

"Stay by me. You may learn something."

Relief broke over the lad's face. "I see what it is. You're going to let him win it back for the sake of his family."

"Good God, Charles! Of course not! What put that maggot in your head?"

The Honorable Charles gritted his teeth. "If it was me, I'd arrange to lose."

"If it was you, you wouldn't need to arrange it," Lord Rupert said brutally. "You're the worst player I've ever known."

The cards were dealt. Silence fell again. The watchers saw Bembridge's eyes light up, and with a sigh of relief he laid down four kings.

Lord Rupert looked him straight in the eyes and smiled. It was only a faint smile, but it was enough to make Bembridge's relief fade and a terrible trembling come over him. Slowly Lord Rupert laid down four aces.

Bembridge struggled up in his chair, his face pale. "You can't do that!" he cried.

"And yet, you see, I have."

"No man could manage that without help."

The change in Lord Rupert's expression was like the unsheathing of a blade. "Are you calling me a cheat?" he asked in a voice as soft as it was deadly.

Bembridge was beyond reason. "I'm calling you worse than that. We all know the power that helps you! You'll not get away with it." Frantically he scrabbled for his vowels on the table but a steely hand gripped his wrist.

"Put them down," Rupert said icily. *"I said put them down."*

He never raised his voice, but Bembridge felt the terror welling up from the pit of his stomach. He wanted to scream, but no sound would come. His legs gave way beneath him and he fell back into his chair.

"That's better," Lord Rupert said. "Now, I want a paper pledging your house."

"My lord—" Bembridge almost sobbed.

"Do it!"

It took some fortification with brandy before he could write the words and hand over the paper. He was helped from his seat and taken into the next room, in a state of collapse. The men around Lord Rupert, all hardened gamblers, regarded him with consternation. As if by a signal they began to edge away, as though avoiding some fearful thing. At last only Charles was left.

Without paying the others the slightest heed Rupert took an envelope, stuffed all the vowels and pledges into it, then wrote a few lines.

"This should be sent to Mrs. Bembridge at once," he observed. "She must be in a fever of anxiety."

Looking over his shoulder, the Honorable Charles read:

Madam, Burn these before your husband returns. Never let him know.

22

"I knew I wasn't mistaken in you," the younger man said in delight. "You're a prime gun."

Lord Rupert winced. "If you're going to talk nonsense, I'm going."

"But why couldn't you have done it my way?"

"First, because a more nauseatingly sentimental idea I never heard. Second, because Bembridge would have promptly gambled the lot away again."

"May I take these to her?" Charles asked eagerly. "They shouldn't be entrusted to a servant."

"You may indeed. It's hardly something I can do myself. And, Charles, not a word, mind. If I find you've disclosed this to anyone my revenge will be terrible."

"Going to turn me into a frog?" the young man said, grinning.

"Much worse. I shall use a really powerful spell and turn you into a sensible, sober man, a credit to your family."

"I say! No need to be that hard on a fellow!"

The Aylesburys were away from Bath for two weeks, and at last the incredible news began to leak out. Lady Jellineck had been wrong in her assessment of George Aylesbury's fate. To put the matter in her own blunt words, the music had stopped. What's more, it had stopped while Toby's name was on the will. Despite the cries and lamentations of the rest of the family, he was the heir to twenty thousand pounds.

When Calvina heard this she fled to her room, threw herself down on her knees, and prayed for the grace not to be glad a man was dead. But it was difficult when so many enchanting images were chasing through her head. Toby, free to marry, home soon, demanding her hand. A few more weeks and her misery would be at an end.

She began counting the days until his return, keeping a watch on herself lest the Dalrymples suspect her joy. A week slipped by. Then another. Christmas came and went. Lady Jellineck gave a party at which she explained

Toby's continued absence by saying that George Aylesbury's affairs were tangled, but his estate was probably worth even more than anyone had suspected. Toby would return to Bath a very warm man.

December passed into January. One night Calvina was awoken by fierce banging on her door. Eglantine stood outside, in a fury. "I've been knocking for ages," she snapped. "My grandmother could die for all you care. The heart drops she keeps by her bed are finished. Where is the other bottle?"

"But there isn't another," Calvina said. "I offered to buy some and she told me to wait until she said so."

"Well, you're in trouble now," Eglantine said spitefully, and rushed away.

Calvina hurriedly threw a shawl over her nightdress and went to Sarah's room. The old woman was gasping dramatically, yet Calvina noticed that her color was good, and she had enough breath to hurl a tirade at her.

"You want me to die," she screeched. "Where are the drops I told you to get?"

"Indeed, madam—" Calvina broke off hopelessly.

"I hope you won't try to defend your conduct," Hugh declared loftily. "Your time would be better spent in fetching medicine from the apothecary."

"But it's nearly three in the morning," she protested.

"Let that be a lesson to you to do what you're told in future."

"Surely James could go—"

Hugh sniffed. "James is employed as a footman," he said grandly, although James actually did any odd job that needed doing. "It is not his responsibility to care for my mother. It is yours."

Calvina said no more, but her mind seethed at the injustice. No respectable woman went out alone, especially at this hour, when the gaming houses would be disgorging their clients. Eglantine would never be sent out like this.

She hurriedly put on her black stuff dress. At the last

24

moment some instinct made her pin the pearl brooch to her chemise, carefully hidden beneath the buttons that reached up to the neck. She'd recently taken to wearing it when she went out, lest it should vanish from her room while she was gone.

She hurried away down the length of Monmouth Street, toward the town center. The lamps in the taverns were still burning brightly, and young men in various stages of rowdiness were tumbling out. Calvina drew back into the shadows until they'd passed, then scuttled away, praying not to be seen.

The apothecary's shop was shuttered and in darkness. Calvina used the knocker and stood back, glancing up and down the street. In the distance she could hear tipsy singing, growing nearer.

At last the apothecary appeared, annoyed at being roused so late. Grumpily he supplied the drops and almost shoved her out into the street, slamming and locking the door behind her. Calvina began to hurry away but found her way blocked by a large man.

"Not so fast, sweetheart," he said, blowing wine fumes over her. "Where are you going so late?"

A man behind Calvina said, "Cyrus has all the luck," and she realized, with horror, that she was surrounded. She tried to dodge away but three men closed in on her. Someone said, "Come on, Cyrus. Don't keep her to yourself."

"Please sir, let me pass." She pulled her hood lower to hide her face.

"Don't be in such a hurry," said the one called Cyrus. "I'm in the mood for adventure. Let's see what you look like."

Calvina felt her hood yanked off from behind, and there was a roar of approval as her face was revealed.

"Well, there's a pretty pullet," Cyrus declared. "Off to meet a lover, eh? But you have three fine lovers right here. You need no other."

She tried to scream but a large, hairy hand went over

25

her mouth, nauseating her. One of the three felt about at her throat, hooked his fingers into her dress, and yanked. The material gave way, revealing her chemise and the shape of her full breasts. Greedy eyes gleamed at her. Calvina was half fainting with fear and disgust, but she managed a spirited kick. Cyrus laughed.

"A lively one. I like that. We'll have some fun tonight, boys. Hey, what's this?" He'd seen the pearl, and his thick, sweaty fingers groped for it. Calvina fought like a wild thing but she was no match for her assailants, and her head was swimming.

She barely heard the sound of carriage wheels on the cobbles, the oath as a man jumped out and sprinted toward them. The hands vanished from her bosom and there was a grunt of pain as Cyrus was slammed back against the wall with a steel fist in his stomach.

Suddenly there was nobody holding Calvina. She grasped the wall and staggered to her feet, trying to force herself to be alert. In the darkness she couldn't make out details, only that one man had taken on the three of them. With Cyrus slumped down making retching noises, her rescuer was handling the other two very efficiently. They were his size but slack bodied and dizzy with drink.

There was something eerie in the efficient ruthlessness with which he dispatched his two opponents, planting fierce blows wherever he pleased on their bodies, winding one, dealing with the other, then returning to the first, almost without a breath. Once Calvina glimpsed his face, and its bloodless, cold-eyed concentration frightened her almost as much as her attackers had done.

Cyrus hauled himself to his feet, his eyes full of malevolence. From somewhere he'd picked up a loose stone, and he raised it to bring it down on the stranger's head. Calvina cried out a warning, but he was too absorbed to hear it. It was left to the coachman to lean down and slip the butt end of his whip over Cyrus's head, clasping it in two hands and hauling him back against the coach. Cyrus gasped and struggled, but he was helpless with the heavy butt pressing against his throat.

In the same moment her rescuer raised his arms, each fist connecting with a chin. As his two opponents slipped limply to the ground, he turned and saw Cyrus fighting to free himself.

"Let him go, Henry," he said. "I can't finish him off while you hold him. It's not sporting."

The coachman released Cyrus so suddenly that he almost fell again. Iron fingers grasped his neck cloth, holding him up while he yammered with fear at something he'd seen in the stranger's eyes.

"Three of you against one woman," the man said in a voice of dreadful quietness. "Hardly fair odds. It's time you had a lesson in manners." Three cold blows brought Cyrus to his knees, and it was all over.

The stranger turned to Calvina, and her eyes opened wide as she saw who her rescuer was. "You!" she whispered.

"Lord Rupert Glennister at your service, ma'am. Get in and I'll take you home. Where is it?"

"Monmouth Street," she said in a shaking voice.

He steadied her as she climbed into the carriage. Calvina's mind was whirling. This man had saved her, yet he'd done so in such a way that she could really believe he was the devil. A small lantern hung in the carriage. As it swung it sent dancing shadows over his face, giving him the look of a satyr.

"Your mistress must be a very unreasonable woman to send you out at this hour," he observed.

"I'm not a servant," she said with a touch of bitterness. "At least a servant gets paid. Could you please pull the window down? I'm feeling a little—" Dizziness overcame her. Her head hit the side and the hand that had been holding the edges of her cloak together fell away.

Lord Rupert yanked down the window and supported her with his arms. As he looked down at her lying against his shoulder, he took in everything: her face, her swelling

27

bosom, almost completely revealed, and the pearl brooch. "By Jove!" he said softly.

Calvina's cheeks burned with shame. "How dare you!" she exclaimed. "Let me go this instant."

He immediately released her and moved a few inches away. She hastily covered herself, avoiding his eyes. "I must thank you, sir," she began, "for coming to my aid—"

"Leave that," he said with a shrug. "It's a bore. You did me a service. The evening was devilishly short of entertainment until then."

The cool irony in his voice repelled her and she shrank back into the shadows, pulling the edges of her dress together. Yet she felt as if it were useless to cover herself. Those piercing eyes could look through material to her naked body beneath.

"What possessed you to be out alone at this hour?" he asked harshly. "I thought you were a serving wench, but you're not, not with that educated voice and that pearl. And now I recall where I've seen you before. You were in that carriage that passed my house one night. Who was that ninny acting the tragedy queen?"

"Eglantine Dalrymple."

He gave a crack of laughter. "I know the name, Dalrymple. Don't tell me you're related to the 'saintly' Hugh?"

"No," Calvina said fiercely. "But he calls himself my benefactor. He took me in when my father died, but I'm a drudge, expected to work like a slave and be grateful for being abused and insulted. He pretends to be religious, but my father was a man of true religion. People would come to our house from far and wide to discuss his books, and when he preached the church was always full, because he was loved and respected."

"Who was your father?"

"The Reverend Calvin Bracewell," Calvina said proudly.

"Ah, yes! He was at Oxford, while I was a student."

"You heard him preach?" Calvina asked eagerly.

"Not I. I was being sent down for some piece of youthful folly, and my mind was somewhat occupied. Besides, I didn't often find my way into churches."

His voice died suddenly. A movement of the lantern had thrown its rays on her face. "By heaven!" he murmured. "A virtuous woman who isn't bracket faced!"

"I beg your pardon!"

"You should be more careful. Your face alone is enough to bring you trouble."

"You mean the kind of trouble you rescued me from?"

"No, I mean this kind," he said roughly, pulling her into his arms.

At first she was too startled to resist, and then she knew there was no way of resisting this man. What he wanted, he took, and his arms enclosed her in a grip of steel, while his lips descended on hers with a purpose that would not be denied.

"No," she gasped. "No—"

"Come," he mocked her. "Don't tell me you prefer those ruffians. You'll find me far more skilled."

He covered her mouth again before she could reply, and Calvina felt a dark, swirling excitement begin to rise in her. His lips were warm and firm, teasing hers in subtle ways that sent forks of shocking excitement through her. Now she was sure he was in league with the devil, for the fires of hell burned in his kiss, enthralling her, luring her to perdition.

She made a final, frantic effort to escape temptation. "Release me, my lord," she begged. "Let me out of this carriage."

"And leave you alone in the streets, to fall into some other man's hands?"

"Better any other man's hands but yours," she gasped.

He laughed softly, and she felt his hot breath against her mouth. "You little ignoramus. You know nothing of the matter. Besides, I've never kissed a virtuous woman before, and I revel in new experiences."

He dropped his head, trailing burning lips down her

neck, to her throat with its madly beating pulse. Calvina moaned at the shattering sensations that were coursing through her. She wanted to cry out to him to stop, but the words wouldn't come. She knew she should struggle, but she had no strength. Her body was filled with a delicious fever that left her weak and trembling.

In a dream she felt his kiss go lower, to her exposed breasts. She gasped with shame at this scandalous proceeding, yet his caresses were so sweet, filling her with searing excitement.

"No"—she breathed—"no." But the words were false. Every fiber of her being said yes.

She was a sinner, for how else could she find this fierce delight in his ravishment of her breasts? Only bad women enjoyed such sensations. She was abandoned, lost, drowning in forbidden pleasure, longing for it to end, longing for it to last forever.

She'd been taken over by a terrible power that made her flesh disobey the dictates of her mind. Through no will of her own she found herself sliding her hand behind his head and pulling him closer, arching against him, offering herself shamelessly to his caresses. And he gave those with the devil's own skill, touching her subtly in ways that compelled her to respond. For a few wild moments nothing mattered but to be here, in this man's arms, wholly given up to the sensations of the flesh.

"Aye, you're virtuous," he growled, "if to be ignorant is to be virtuous. No man has ever touched you like this before, has he?"

"No," she exclaimed.

"And yet you were made for the joys of the flesh. Passion can bring you alive as nothing else ever has—or ever will."

"You lie," she said desperately. "I am a true daughter of the church. My faith will protect me from carnal desires."

"Your lips say otherwise when they are on mine. I could make your whole beautiful body say the same, if I

30

had only time. But, alas, there is no time! They'll marry you off to some wooden oaf who'll never appreciate you. He'll take his own pleasure, caring nothing for yours. And you'll bed him dutifully and never know your true destiny. So this is all we can share, and we must enjoy it while we can."

He kissed her again with a purpose and insistence that made the blood pound in her veins. What he said was monstrous, wicked, and yet . . .

"The carriage is slowing," he announced in a voice that wasn't quite steady. "I perceive that we've reached Monmouth Street. The number?"

Half-insensible, she whispered it. A moment later they halted. Without asking her consent Lord Rupert wrapped her in his cloak, gathered her up in his arms as if she weighed nothing, and went up the steps to the door that was already being pulled open.

Lights were on in the hall and the entire family was there to witness the staggering sight of Calvina being carried in by the devil. Hugh, in dressing gown and slippers, held a candle high to see if his eyes deceived him.

"Where can I put her?" Rupert demanded. "Quick man, don't stand there gobbling like a turkey."

Puffing with outrage at being thus addressed, Hugh indicated a sofa by the wall. Rupert lay Calvina gently down and turned to face the others. In the flickering candlelight his face was at its most satanic.

"Oh, Ma!" Eglantine shrieked, and cast herself on her mother's scrawny bosom. "Save me!"

"Calm yourself, madam," Rupert ordered her sardonically. "It ain't my day for ravishin' females. That's Thursdays, and then strictly by appointment."

"I shall faint, I shall faint," Eglantine moaned.

"Not on this floor, I hope," he said, surveying his dim surroundings with distaste. "Needs cleaning."

"Sir!" Maria drew herself up to her full height. "Your foul jest is one no decent woman should hear. But I fear nothing. I defy you."

Hugh muttered, "Noble woman," but Rupert ignored him.

"Wasted effort, ma'am, I do assure you," he told Maria. "You were never in any danger. Now"—ignoring Maria's gasp of outrage, he faced Hugh—"I found Miss Bracewell being attacked by ruffians. What were you thinking of to send a gently-bred lady out unprotected?"

Hugh sniffed. "Gently bred is as gently does," he declared.

"I'll give you two seconds to explain what you mean by that foolish remark," Rupert said icily.

Two centuries wouldn't have been enough and Hugh knew it. He merely gobbled and puffed.

"As I thought," Rupert said. "Stupid as well as ill-bred."

"I? Ill-bred?"

"No man of breeding would have sent Miss Bracewell out alone at this hour. Nor would he have made a drudge of her on the pretext of offering her a home."

"Lies! Spiteful lies!" Hugh shouted. "I've been a father to that ungrateful young woman. I gave her a roof. I pray for her night and day." He dropped to his knees. "Oh Lord, hear thy servant's plea! Cleanse this house from the pollution of this man's presence. Protect us, Lord."

Maria, Sarah, and Eglantine also dropped down, raising their arms to join in the chorus of "Protect us, Lord."

"Miss Bracewell," Rupert addressed Calvina, who was trying to force her head to clear, "I must leave you now."

"Save us from the man who is thy foe . . ." Hugh roared.

"Protect us, Lord!"

"I hope you will take no serious hurt from this night's events."

"Thank you, sir," she faltered.

"Protect us, Lord!"

"May I say in passing, Miss Bracewell, that you have my deepest sympathy?" Without a backward glance he strode to the door and vanished into the night.

"We thank thee," Hugh cried, "that thou has shown us thy favor by smiting the rogue and sending him fleeing from our house, fearful and ashamed."

"But he saved me—" Calvina protested.

Hugh raised his voice. "Take pity on thy handmaiden, that the evil one may not have besmirched her."

Calvina pulled herself up, indignation overcoming all other feelings. "I wouldn't have met 'the evil one' if you hadn't sent me out alone," she pointed out. "You would never have treated Eglantine so."

"Her mind has been polluted," Hugh howled, "so that she turns on her protectors. Save her from sin! Chastise her with scorpions so that she may become thy child again."

Something in the frozen silence told him that he no longer had anyone's attention. Lord Rupert had reappeared in the door and addressed Calvina.

"Forgive me, but I left my cloak behind."

Dazed, she gave it to him, and he turned away. But at the door he looked back for a moment, taking in the scene he'd interrupted. A derisive grin twisted his mouth. Then he was gone.

Eglantine collapsed in hysterics, and her mother fussed about her. Hugh took Calvina's arm in a grip of iron. "Let me assist you to your room," he said, but his tone was as cold as his piggy eyes.

He half dragged her up the three flights of stairs and into her tiny room. He thrust her inside, kicked the door shut, and slapped her hard across the face.

"I'll teach you manners, miss," he said viciously. "Making shame of us all with your wanton ways. Attacked by ruffians, were you? I know the kind of ruffians your sort attracts. Bringing a man of evil repute to this house and telling him lies about us."

Calvina backed against the wall. "I told no lies," she said in a shaking but determined voice. "It's true that you make a slave of me—" She broke off with a scream as he slapped her again.

"And I say it's a lie," he raged. "You've had nothing but comfort and good living since I took you in, and it's spoiled you. But those days are over, my fine lady. You'll live in sackcloth and ashes until you repent your sin. We'll see how proud you are then."

He aimed another blow but Calvina covered her face with both hands. Too late she remembered that one of them had been holding her dress together, and tried to seize it again, but Hugh had seen the brooch, and the next moment he yanked it from her.

"So that's where—" he began unguardedly but recovered himself quickly. "It's devotion to earthly things that's been your undoing. Jewels ruineth the soul, and the salvation of your soul is my duty."

He turned but Calvina threw herself at him in a frenzy of pleading. "No," she sobbed. "It was my mother's. It's all I have of hers . . . for pity's sake don't take it . . ."

"The devil is cunning to put such arguments in your mouth. But I am more cunning than the devil, for I have the strength of heaven. With its help I will teach you to spurn baubles."

"No," she screamed, *"I beg of you! . . ."*

But Hugh threw her to the floor and the next thing she heard was the sound of the key turning in the lock.

No one visited her the next day, and by the following day she was ill with hunger and thirst. Some sour water was provided and a morsel of bread. Thereafter she was fed tiny meals, twice a day.

Hugh would come in the early morning to force her to kneel on the cold floor while he prayed over her. To others his behavior might have seemed pious, but to Calvina, bred in true religion by a gentle, compassionate man, Hugh's "prayers" were a farcical blasphemy. But she was forced to play her part, on pain of being left without food or water. Sometimes she would venture to plead for the return of her brooch, but this merely inspired him to fervent declamations about her covetous

34

heart, and the prayers would be redoubled until she fainted.

By day she had nothing to do but read the "improving works" Hugh left her. They were pamphlets of appalling, sentimental religiosity written by Hugh, and they sickened her.

Her attic room was high up and set at an angle, so that she could just glimpse the front door, and that was how she knew of Toby's visit. She rapped on the window, calling to him, but he couldn't hear, and she saw him vanish into the house. An hour later she witnessed his departure and threw herself onto the bed in despair.

Her evening meal, such as it was, was brought by Eglantine. She, too, would make Calvina wait while she gossiped spitefully about her days, emphasizing the delightful time she was having.

"Ma's told everyone that you've gone to the seaside for your health," she said.

"In this cold weather?" Calvina asked.

Eglantine shrugged. "Toby asked your exact direction, so I'm afraid"—Eglantine sighed regretfully—"I'm afraid we were forced to tell him the truth about your scandalous behavior. He was very much shocked. Pa had to exhort him for an hour before he could be consoled. You quite shattered his faith in female nature. He took us to visit his sainted mama today. Of course, the family is in mourning since their tragic bereavement."

Calvina could imagine what the Dalrymples had told Toby, but surely he hadn't been deceived by it? He knew her sufferings at their hands, and his love would never fail her. She was so certain that he was merely biding his time, that she fixed her thoughts on that glorious future when she would be Toby's wife.

The weather grew even colder. Starved and chilled, she fell victim to a fever. Her treatment improved slightly. Evidently the Dalrymples felt her death would be an embarrassment. So there were warm blankets and better food, except that she was too ill to eat it.

The devil wandered through her fevered dreams, with his piercing eyes and cruel smile. Yet it was his powerful presence that protected her. Sometimes she was back in the coach, feeling her body burn and her limbs grow weak as he kissed her in a way no decent woman could remember without shame. She was hot and trembling still, but whether with sickness or the memory of that dark, flaming moment she didn't know.

Then she would be in the hallway, listening to Lord Rupert sparring with her tormentors. She'd barely listened at the time, but every word was in her mind now. With what cool wit had he demolished Hugh's pretensions and exposed Eglantine's foolishness! There was something in his tough, ironic mind that pleased her, despite his dreadful reputation. But why, oh why had he repeated her frank words about the Dalrymples? That had been the moment when their dislike of her had gone beyond reason.

At last the fever departed, and she woke. A fire burned in the grate, and Eglantine tended her with apparent good will. It was several days before she recovered enough to ask questions. With a self-satisfied smile Eglantine explained.

"Pa says your suffering has purged the sin from you, and you may be present at a party we're giving on Friday."

So that was it. Her absence was causing questions, and Hugh was putting her on show to silence tongues. But at least she would escape from her room. And Toby might be there. She could beg him to take her away at once. She fell asleep dreaming of him.

On the night of the party she was still shaky, but managed to attire herself in her gray silk, with Toby's locket about her neck. When he saw it he would know her heart was still his.

When she saw the first carriage through her tiny window she began to descend, but Maria barred her way and told her sharply to return to her room until she was summoned. Calvina did so, and an hour later Maria rapped on her door, demanding to know why she was keeping everyone waiting.

She made her solitary way downstairs. On the turn of a landing she encountered herself in a long mirror and was shocked. How thin she'd grown! And how large her eyes were in her pale face.

Hugh was waiting in the hall. "I want no trouble from you, miss," he informed her curtly. "This is a family celebration. You'll offer your congratulations, smile, and depart. Now take my arm."

She shrank back, but he seized her hand and drew it through his arm. Through the open doors Calvina could see a blaze of light. The room was packed with finely-dressed people. After the dreariness of her room she found the light too harsh and blinked.

"Calvina has been very poorly," Hugh declared, "and she won't stay with us long. But she insisted on leaving her sickbed to bless the happy couple."

There was a murmur of approval. Calvina glided forward as if in a dream. There was Eglantine dressed up like a tinsel doll, her face full of malicious triumph. One pudgy hand displayed a large engagement ring. The other kept a fearful grip on a young man by her side, while he—oh, it couldn't be true!

Eglantine's promised husband was Toby.

Calvina stood rooted to the spot, her features a mask of despair and disbelief. Horror dawned in Toby's eyes as he read the truth in her face.

"Won't you congratulate us, sister?" Eglantine cried. She squeezed Toby's arm and rattled on, "Calvina is so dear to me that I call her sister, and now she will be your sister, too."

"I—nothing could please me more—" he managed to say in a strangled voice. "You look so pale—a seat—some champagne—"

She let him guide her to a small sofa by the wall. The Dalrymples didn't try to stop their talking apart. The

37

battle was won. There was more pleasure in watching Calvina's dawning comprehension.

"So you really believed I'd acted dishonorably?" she said in a low, bitter voice. "How *could* you think that?"

"I don't understand you," he said. "I came here to beg your hand in marriage, but they told me you'd left the house to escape my 'odious advances,' that you'd turned your back on the world to live a life of religion."

"I've been imprisoned here for weeks. I thought you would come for me—I longed for you—"

"And I for you," he said wretchedly. "I came every day in the hope of news. Eglantine would speak of you so sweetly and—we talked. Then Hugh said I'd compromised her—that she'd be ruined if I didn't marry her. Oh, my darling, what can we do?"

For a moment hope blazed. They'd found each other again, and their love was as pure and bright as it had always been. Then joy faded as they faced the terrible truth. "There's nothing we can do, Toby. Your betrothal has been announced. As a man of honor you can't go back."

"They tricked me with a lie," he burst out in a fierce whisper. "At least, Hugh did. I'm sure Eglantine had no part in it. Now I've given her my word, but it's you I love."

"And I you. I shall love you forever, but it's all over. We can never be together."

Hugh's voice was raised in ear-splitting joviality. "It's time to toast the happy pair," Hugh cried. "Toby, my dear boy, come and take the hand of your beautiful bride-to-be in yours."

Dazed, he complied. Calvina watched him stand beside his future wife, saw Eglantine regard him with a possessive glee that held no shred of tenderness.

And then, suddenly, everything seemed to vanish from the room, leaving Calvina's eyes fixed on one shocking sight.

Eglantine was wearing her pearl brooch.

"My brooch," she said in a choking voice. "You've stolen my brooch."

A gasp rose from the assembled company, but Hugh kept his composure. "Your illness has affected your mind, dear Calvina. Can you have forgotten that you gave Eglantine your brooch as a betrothal gift? How it touched my heart to hear your words on that occasion—"

Calvina's anger rose and threatened to engulf her. She had borne much, but suddenly could bear no more. Like a lioness at bay she turned on her tormentors.

"Liar!" she cried. "You are liars and hypocrites, all of you. You preach religion, but you are cruel and greedy. Now you are thieves, too, but I won't let you—"

She darted forward, her hands outstretched to tear the brooch from Elgantine, but Hugh seized her and yanked her away. His smile was ghastly.

"How tragic—her mind—subject to attacks—long rest and complete seclusion—"

"No!" Calvina screamed. "You shan't imprison me again!"

"For your own good, dear," Hugh said through gritted teeth. "Until the spirit of madness leaves you—help me, Maria."

His wife seized Calvina's other arm. Dread of being taken to the attic again had sent the strength flooding back to Calvina's limbs and she was struggling like a wild thing. Old Mrs. Dalrymple surged after them, determined not to miss the fun. In the melee her wig was knocked sideways.

"Hold her down," Hugh gasped. "She's possessed by demons."

"No, *you* are the demon." Calvina's eyes flashed at him. But she could feel that they were too much for her. She was being forced inexorably to the stairs. Once in the attic she would be lost.

The knocker thundered. James, doing duty as porter, pulled the door open. The Dalrymples froze, staring at their newly arrived guests. Calvina seized the moment, lashing out with arms and legs until she was free, and darting out of the door into the darkness. A cry of "Stop her!" floated from the house, but she was soon lost in the night.

Chapter Three

She stumbled blindly down the street, driven by fear and anger. People stared but she didn't see them. All that mattered was to get far away, no matter where, so that the Dalrymples couldn't find her.

After what seemed like ages she stopped for breath and recognized her surroundings. This was Barton Street where she'd first glimpsed Lord Rupert Glennister leaving his house. What instinct had brought her to the man who'd caused so much of her misfortune?

There was the house. Calvina staggered up to the front door and knocked wildly, then leaned, half collapsing, against the wall, until the door opened, and an elderly footman appeared. Only years of training kept his face blank as he regarded the bedraggled creature before him.

"I must speak to Lord Rupert," she said, gasping.

"May I ask your business with his lordship?"

"He has ruined me," Calvina said fiercely.

"Who is it?" Rupert's voice came from the shadows.

"A young person, my lord." The footman added tonelessly, "She says your lordship has ruined her."

"The devil she does!"

A step, and he appeared. The footman tactfully withdrew. Rupert was finely dressed as though preparing to entertain or be entertained and looked even more wolfishly handsome than she remembered. He stared at Calvina without recognition but pulled her in out of the cold.

"I don't know who you are or what you—good grief, yes I do! The parson's daughter."

"I suppose I should be lucky you remember me," she said bitterly.

"What do you mean by saying I ruined you? If you think one kiss means ruin you're a bigger innocent than I thought. Besides, nobody knew, unless you told them."

"They saw you carry me into the house," she cried. "And you told them what I said. All my wrongs since then have sprung from that."

"Then you'd better tell me. But don't take long. I'm expecting guests. Here." He'd urged her before him into a room with a dining table, set for supper. There were four places, each set with the best crystal and silver. The sideboard groaned with food. Fine wines stood already uncorked.

He poured some into a heavy goblet and handed it to her. She gulped it down and held out the empty glass, which made him raise an eyebrow in sardonic amusement.

"Only one more," he said, filling the glass. "I doubt you're used to wine, especially of this quality. Have the Dalrymples been making themselves unpleasant?"

"They locked me up after you left. They starved me, stole the only thing I treasured, but I endured it all—for Toby's sake."

"And just who is Toby?"

"He's the man I was to marry." She choked. "I love him, and he loves me. But they —they stole him, too."

"How did they do that?" Lord Rupert sounded bored.

"They told him I'd gone away to escape him. He thought it was all over between us. I was allowed downstairs tonight—*to celebrate his betrothal to Eglantine*. She was wearing my mother's brooch—they said I'd given it to her—that my mind was wandering. It was a lie. They tried to imprison me again, but I ran away."

"Wise of you," Lord Rupert said curtly.

"Except that I've nowhere to go."

42

"It seems you've come to me."

"That was by chance. I ran without looking, and somehow found myself here. Now I'm leaving." She began to rise.

"Sit down," he said calmly. "You showed spirit and sense when you fled that place. Don't spoil it by having the vapors now."

Calvina's head went up. "I never have the vapors. I'll survive. I'll be a governess."

He gave a crack of laughter. "You? A governess?"

"Let me tell you, sir, that I've been well taught by my father. I know Latin and Greek, mathematics, science—"

"In other words you're totally unfit to instruct young girls in ladylike nothings. No family would have you." Without warning he took her chin in his fingers and turned her face to him. "Especially when they saw that angel face."

"How dare you—"

He laughed. "Prudish? After what we shared?"

Her face flamed. "You shouldn't—no gentleman would—"

"But I'm no gentleman. I'm the devil. Haven't they told you? Take my word about your face. I'm an expert on women's looks. You may be a parson's daughter, but you're designed to tempt a man to perdition. That's what the wives and mothers will think. You won't even get through the door."

"I'll never go back to the Dalrymples," she said passionately.

"Why should you? Having escaped them and the useless Toby . . ."

"It wasn't his fault—"

"A man who could let himself be duped out of one bride and into another is worth nothing," Lord Rupert said contemptuously. "If I wanted a woman I'd break down the doors and put a knife through anyone who tried to stop me."

"Toby isn't like that. He's gentle and kind—"

"Spare me the nauseating details. He sounds a milk-sop. You're better off without him."

"I love him," she cried.

"And you blame me?"

"Partly. I'm grateful to you for saving me, but you should have let me out of the carriage to walk the last few yards. Why did you insist on kissing me?"

He shrugged. "Because I wanted to kiss you, and that's the best reason I know for doing anything."

"No matter whom you harm?" She flung the words at him bitterly.

There was an odd, arrested look in his eyes. "Have I harmed you? Very well, I'll make amends. Our marriage can take place immediately."

"How dare you make fun of me!"

He was strangely pale. "This is no joke. I need a virtuous wife, and you will be ideal."

"You know nothing about me."

"I know a good deal, including your kinship to Lord Stoneham. After our meeting I made it my business to find out about you."

"But why?"

He shrugged. "I thought you might be useful to me. You'd better know that my excesses have shocked polite society once too often. Only a good woman can win me the entrée again. You'll suit my purpose admirably. By God, I can't wait to see their faces when I walk in with a parson's daughter. Nothing could suit me better."

Calvina forced herself to her feet and faced him. "I think you must have taken leave of your senses," she said stormily.

He shrugged. "Why should you refuse? I offer you a life of luxury and ease. In return your virtue will be my passport back to the ton."

"Are the people of the ton so admirable that you must be accepted by them at such a price?"

"Admirable? My dear little innocent, they're a parcel

44

of empty-headed nodcocks moved only by greed, money, and rank. The women are stupid, the men disgusting."

"Then why do you seek their society?"

"Because they have excluded me," he said in a voice like cold silk. "That collection of dolts and dummies has dared to say that they will have none of me. Of *me*!" Like lightning his expression changed, becoming black with rage. "There's hardly a titled lady who hasn't come after me like a bitch in heat, slavering to get me into her bed. I've sat opposite the men with cards in my hand that spelt their doom, and watched them gamble away one thing after another because they were weak-willed fools. I've seen them sodden with drink, pouring out their family wealth on mistresses who laughed at them. And now they dare to judge *me* and tell me I'm not good enough for them."

For a moment he was truly frightening, and Calvina felt the hairs begin to stand up on her head. He spoke as one who knew the depths of sin. But Papa had taught her to defy sin, not to fear it. "You scorn them, but you're like them," she challenged him.

"Don't dare to say that."

"Don't you, too, gamble heavily?"

"Very heavily, but never beyond my means, and I seldom lose."

The wine was affecting her now. She eyed him boldly. "I wonder why, my lord."

"So you've heard the rumors? Well, believe what you like. I'm accountable to no one."

"And the—other things you mentioned? Are you so different?"

"I enjoy women. I take what's offered and pay for it, but no woman has ever been in a position to laugh at me. I stole a kiss from you but no more. If it harmed you— well, I'm ready to make amends."

"It's horrible," she cried. "I can't possibly marry you."

"Can't you, Calvina? Do you find me distasteful then?"

His eyes mocked her, knowing the answer. She'd responded wildly to his kiss, but only a man without principles would ask such a shameless question while she was in his power. She turned away, pressing her hands to her burning cheeks, but he seized them and held them fast.

"Answer me," he commanded. "Tell me to my face that your flesh is cold to me."

She met his eyes and tried to speak steadily. "That was—an aberration. I've heard of your powers. You cast a dark spell on me."

He gave her a smile that made her heart beat faster. The remembered heat began to steal over her body. It was wicked, and she knew she must fight it, but she was helpless.

"But that's what passion is, Calvina," he murmured. "A dark spell that bewitches two people. For those few moments I was as spellbound as you." He lifted her chin with his fingers, and this time there was no escape. She felt herself melting at the look in his eyes, and the soft brush of his lips against hers.

"No," she breathed. "Temptation is—the work of the devil—"

"But I am the devil," he whispered. "You know that. My spells can fire you with the pleasure of life as your Toby's never did."

"Toby is a gentleman—he would never dream of—"

"Just as I thought," he mocked. "A milksop. I'll wager you had to be content with a peck on the cheek. Did it make your heart race, like this—and like this—?"

She found the strength to pull away from him. "Do you always take exactly what you want, my lord?" she demanded.

"Sometimes. On other occasions it's more amusing to make people give it to me."

"You think I'm mere food for amusement?" she raged.

"Did I say that I meant you? Well, perhaps a little. But there'll be more between us than amusement, Calvina.

46

Lust is a blunt instrument, and you deserve something more delicate. What a duel there'll be between us! How we will both enjoy it!

"For the moment I'll respect your sensibilities and make no demands on you. Later we'll have to produce an heir, but I can bide my time." His eyes raked her down, seeming to see right through her dress, making her feel naked.

"Pleasure deferred has a piquancy of its own," he mused. "To begin with, we won't interfere with each other's lives. I trust your father's daughter as I would trust no other, and you can enjoy yourself as you please. I think that's a fair bargain."

Calvina pulled herself together. "It is no bargain, my lord, because I'll have no part of it."

In a moment he changed. The mockery left his voice and his eyes, leaving only chill courtesy. "Very well, madam. I'll summon my carriage. You can give the coachman your direction."

"You'd send me back to *them*?"

"Not at all. Henry will take you anywhere you like."

His cool eyes met her horrified ones. There could be no appeal to this man's pity. He would save her—but on his own terms.

"You'd marry me, knowing that I'm in love with another man?"

"Have I asked for your love? It plays no part in our bargain."

"But why me? Isn't there some lady who has your heart—?"

"Don't talk like a ninny," he said harshly. "I have no heart, and I don't seek one in you. I've never fallen in love with a woman, and if I did she'd be the last person I'd marry. Fair exchange is the best that can be hoped for from your sex, and a man seldom finds even that much honesty. And don't imagine that you're going to reform me. I marry you to continue the life that suits me, not

47

give it up. Now, we've talked long enough. Our marriage must take place tonight."

"Not so fast. I haven't agreed."

"But you have. Don't you realize that the die is already cast? Why else did you come here?"

"I've told you, it was chance—"

"No. Your feet were drawn by a force you don't understand."

"Are you saying you brought me here by black magic?"

"You came to me because you had to, and you know it as well as I do."

She backed away from him into the shadows. Hot, lurid images seemed to surround her. She covered her face but the pictures were still there: wantonness, shocking pleasures, guilty delights. And over them all brooded this man, with the fires of hell glowing behind him.

"Look at me, Calvina."

"No—no—"

He pulled her hands from her face. "Look at me."

Helplessly she complied. His eyes were close to hers. They were all she could see. "There is nothing to be afraid of," he said softly. "You are going to do what I say, because in your heart, that is what you want."

"I have no choice, have I?" she whispered.

"None whatever. We'll be married in a few hours, then I'll take you straight to my home."

"Isn't this your home?"

"No, merely a rented lodging. My home is Glennister Court, a few miles away. Yes, what is it?" A footman had entered. Calvina pulled away and pressed her hands over her burning cheeks while the man murmured something to Lord Rupert.

"I haven't time tonight," he replied impatiently. "Get rid of them. Tell the steward to prepare a room for this lady, then find me a priest. Don't stand there staring, man. I said a priest."

When the footman had gone he said, "You should be

48

tended by a woman, of course, but there are no female servants in this house. I keep it because it's convenient. After tonight you'll forget it exists. You will never mention it to anyone, least of all to me."

He didn't wait for her reply, obviously taking it for granted that she would accede to his wishes. Calvina was dizzy with the speed of events. She seemed to have agreed to this monstrous plan, yet she didn't remember agreeing. She couldn't marry him, but neither could she refuse. In a few minutes Sam, the elderly steward, led her upstairs. At the turn of the stairs she looked down into the hall and saw three young women in gaudy, low-cut gowns. Even to someone with Calvina's modest upbringing, it was obvious what they were. They seemed discontented, until the footman handed them each some money. Then their faces brightened, and they danced out of the front door.

Calvina's mind reeled. There was no doubt which kind of "pleasures" Lord Rupert had meant. But *three*!

Sam showed her into a room with a large bed and took her dress away to brush down. A few minutes later he brought her refreshments, and she realized she was light-headed. She'd expected to lie awake as the hour approached when she must take the fateful step, but she was so exhausted that she fell instantly into a sleep from which Sam awoke her with the words, "His lordship asks you to be ready in half an hour, miss."

The gray dress was slightly improved by the attention it had received. Calvina made her hair neat and orderly, but she knew she cut a strange figure as a bride. Her only adornment was the locket she'd been wearing when she fled the Dalrymples, with Toby's picture inside. How could she wear one man's picture while she wed another? This was insane. She should stop it now. But she seemed to be moving in a dream.

But then a practical thought occurred to her, and when she met Lord Rupert at the foot of the stairs she voiced it.

"We cannot marry tonight, my lord. We need a special license."

"It arrived from the bishop ten minutes ago," he said coolly.

"You awoke him in the middle of the night? And he simply agreed?"

"He owed me money. I had his note for a thousand. He was glad to get it back. Now, if you're ready."

Two men were in the dining room, sitting at the table, which had been cleared. They rose and bowed slightly, and she recognized the older one as a pastor she'd once heard preach in the church the Dalrymples attended. So this was real and not some wicked masquerade: a possibility that had crossed her mind.

"I've known Mr. Bevan since I was a child," Rupert said, introducing them. "He's retired, but still in orders, and has consented to do me this service tonight."

"But only on one condition," the old man interrupted him.

"He wishes to be sure that I'm not forcing you against your will," Lord Rupert said. "You may speak privately in the room next door."

"There's no need," Calvina said. She addressed the clergyman. "I do this of my own free will."

But how true was that, she wondered, when Lord Rupert seemed to have taken possession of her soul?

The other man was a lawyer. He asked her some questions about herself and took notes. Then it was time for the ceremony. Somehow she was standing beside her groom, listening to him say, "I, Rupert James Glennister, do take thee, Calvina Elizabeth Bracewell, to be my lawful wedded wife . . ." His voice was totally without expression. The hand holding hers was strong and warm. She knew that her own hand must feel as cold as the rest of her body.

"I, Calvina Elizabeth Bracewell, do take thee . . ." The ring was too large for her and she supposed it was one of his own. Its weight felt strange on her little hand. She looked up at Rupert, but suddenly it was Toby's face she saw there, and the terrifying rashness of her action swept over her. She'd lost Toby, but he was still the man she loved, and she'd tied herself to a sinister stranger.

The heavy ring marked her as Lord Rupert's property, according to the laws of the land. He could do as he liked with her, use her well or show her no mercy. And she'd walked into the cage like a sleepwalker.

She gave a little gasp and he looked at her sharply. She lowered her lids, hoping he hadn't seen the glint of tears in her eyes, or the dread that flooded her soul as she understood the shocking thing she'd done.

It was still dark when the carriage containing Lord and Lady Rupert Glennister drew away from the house in Barton Street, headed out of Bath for Glennister Court. Already her circumstances had changed, for now she was swathed in a warm cloak, belonging to her husband, with a hot brick at her feet.

They spoke little on the journey. Lord Rupert inquired politely after his bride's comfort, and she declared, truthfully, that everything had been attended to.

Night's blackness was just turning to gray as they reached the estate. At first the road lay through a thick wood. Despite the approach of dawn it was quiet, as though no bird dared to sing here. Involuntarily Calvina shivered.

"There's a bend a mile ahead that will give you your first view of the house," Rupert told her.

"Has it stood there very long?" she asked, unable to think of anything else to say.

"Parts of it go back six hundred years but it's been added to many times, sometimes well, mostly badly. Don't imagine an attractive house, or you'll be disappointed."

"But do you love it? Was it a true home to you?"

He grinned. "It's where I fought all my fiercest battles with my father, if that's what you mean. He was still fighting me on his deathbed."

51

"And your mother?"

"Dead long ago."

"But you must have some family?"

"My aunt Josephine lives with me and my cousin Ninian, who runs the place. I have various other distant kin around the country, but they don't care to know me, and I care nothing for them."

Calvina shivered again, but this time at the bleak picture he painted of his own life.

Suddenly the light grew. They had reached the bend, and she saw Glennister Court. As Rupert had said, it wasn't an attractive house. One part of it still bore signs of the castle it had once been. It was a long, low building, with a strangely sullen air. Here was no happy home to welcome a new bride.

By the time they drew up the sun was starting to appear. Evidently they were expected, for the huge main door was pulled slowly open. Calvina took Rupert's arm and braced herself to meet his aunt Josephine. It sounded a dignified and daunting name, but when she saw the plump, middle-aged lady in a voluminous dressing gown bustling down the wide stairs she felt a little more at ease.

"Rupert, my dear boy, I've had the strangest message. Something about your getting married on the spur of the moment, but, of course, it couldn't be that. Not even you would—"

"But I would, and I have," he said. "Aunt Josie, meet my wife, Calvina."

Shock warred with good nature on Aunt Josie's face, and good nature won. "Welcome, my dear," she said, embracing Calvina. "I don't understand anything, but you look done to death. Come into the warm and have something to eat, because if you've been silly enough to marry my nephew, and I'm sure I don't know why anyone should, you'll need all the comfort you can get."

Rupert grinned at these frank words, but it was bliss to

Calvina to be wrapped in Aunt Josie's kindness. There was soon a fire burning in the library. She was served hot coffee and rolls, with small pots of jam. It was a light meal, but after her recent privations it felt like a feast. While she ate, Rupert drew his aunt aside and must have told her the circumstances, for Josie exclaimed a good deal before swooping on Calvina, enfolding her in a deep embrace, and exclaiming, "You poor, poor dear! I do hope you'll be happy. I'll do my best to make sure everything here is to your liking, but oh, whatever made you do it?"

"Don't make it worse, Aunt," Rupert observed dryly. "She's already convinced she's married a monster."

"And I'm not surprised. I don't know what you were thinking of, you foolish boy. There, my dear, you're tired. I gave orders for a room, and it should be ready by now. The mistress of the house occupies the White Room, but it'll take time to bring it into order, so I've put you in the best guest room, just for now."

"Thank you, ma'am. I should so like to rest. So much has happened . . ."

She was enveloped in kindness, escorted to a comfortable room, undressed by a maid under Josie's supervision, and put to bed between clean sheets that had been thoroughly rubbed with a warming pan. She'd slept for barely two hours at Rupert's house, and she fell asleep again at once and didn't awaken until late afternoon.

Now it seemed as though everything had happened to somebody else, and only the dramatic change in her surroundings confirmed that she had left her old life behind and become Lady Rupert Glennister. The maid came to dress her and coax her hair into a more becoming style. As Calvina went downstairs she wondered what Rupert was thinking now of the step he'd taken. Was he regretting its madness and devising ways to be rid of her? Strangely, she found her heart beating urgently at the thought of seeing him again.

Josie came to meet her, hands outstretched, a warm

smile on her plump face. "There, you look delightful. I told Hanna to do your hair like that, and I was right."

"Did you choose it because Rupert likes it?" Calvina asked shyly.

"Don't mention Rupert's name to me," Josie said, throwing up her hands. "I'm so cross with him. What must he do but dash back to Bath and I don't know when we'll see him again. But never mind. He'll turn up when it suits him, I daresay. In the meantime you can meet Ninian, and the three of us will have a delightful coze over dinner."

Calvina covered her shock with a smile. Rupert had prepared her for no more than such a show of indifference. But what really disturbed her was the little stab of dismay she'd felt when she heard he'd gone.

Josie told her to wait in the library and scurried away on some small errand. Calvina looked with fascination at the tiers of books that lined the high walls. She was at home in a room like this.

She didn't notice the young man perched on some steps, who'd stopped with a book in his hand, arrested by the sight of her. She wandered over to the fire and stood pensively looking into the flames, unaware what a charming picture she presented. A smile touched the young man's gentle mouth, and he descended to greet her in a quiet, pleasant voice.

"Oh!" Calvina turned with a start. "I had no idea anyone was there."

"Forgive me. I shouldn't have watched you while you were unaware, but I was so intrigued to see my cousin's new wife."

"You must be Ninian." Calvina liked what she saw. Ninian was of medium height with mild manners and a quiet voice. He was dressed with neatness and propriety. His only touch of flamboyance was a heavy gold signet ring on his left hand.

"I am. It's an honor to meet you, Lady Rupert."

It was the first time anyone had used her new title, and she flushed. "Please—I'd rather you called me Calvina."

"Thank you," he said gravely. "I understand that your father was Calvin Bracewell. May I say how much I admired him? I heard him preach several times when I was at Oxford, and I have copies of all his works."

"Thank you." Her heart warmed to Ninian. His sincere appreciation of her father was a welcome contrast to the noisy mouthings she'd heard from Hugh.

Josie returned and performed the introductions properly. Ninian joined them for dinner, and Calvina was made to tell the whole story of her life. She managed not to mention Toby, and parts of her life with the Dalrymples she left vague, but the other two seemed to understand for they looked sympathetic.

Calvina found Ninian a delightful companion, with pleasing manners and sensible conversation. But when dinner was over Aunt Josie shooed him away, saying that she and Calvina had urgent matters to discuss that would not interest him.

The urgent matters turned out to be proposed visits to silk warehouses to choose materials for Calvina's new wardrobe. "And in general we must prepare you to enter society as soon as possible," Josie said.

"Me? In society?"

"Of course. Rupert must introduce you to the ton so that they can see for themselves—oh dear! Did he not explain? That is—why did he say he was marrying you?"

"To flaunt my virtue in the face of the world," Calvina said. "Be at ease, ma'am. Nothing could have been more brutally frank than the manner of his proposal. He swore he'd never been in love, even once."

Josie sighed. "I'm afraid that's true. Such a pity! It would do him so much good. Ah well, he is what he is. At least he was candid with you. Well, now you see, you must learn what it means to be part of the ton."

Calvina very soon realized that life with her father had left her sadly short of social accomplishments. She could neither ride a horse nor dance, and her days were to be spent in acquiring these skills, when she wasn't being measured for new clothes.

The first time she saw the bolts of silk, satin, velvet, muslin, bombazine, crepe, and gauze, all laid out for her inspection, Calvina gave a gasp of pure delight. Papa would have shaken his head at such vanity, but surely he would have understood that she was merely doing her duty to her husband? Then she forgot Papa in a whirl of delight.

At last the materials were chosen, the patterns selected, and four seamstresses were piled high with work. Calvina and Josie were exhausted but united by a sense of triumph.

Ninian rapidly became her friend. After dinner Aunt Josie would snooze by the fire while they talked. He'd not only read her father's books but understood them, and it was like coming home to her to be able to discuss points with him. He shyly confessed that he would have liked to take orders.

"But my father used to run the Glennister estates," he said. "When he died Rupert asked me to take over, and I thought it was my duty. He's a strange man, who keeps himself apart, not outwardly, but in a place deep inside him. I don't think anybody knows who he really is in his heart. But he is kind enough to call me friend. I feel I should be near him."

Calvina wondered at something she could sense but which Ninian was plainly unwilling to say. Rupert, with his terrifying reputation, might need this gentle and good man. And Ninian's very friendship must signal to the world that "the devil" wasn't beyond redemption.

He seemed to confirm this view once when they were riding together. Calvina had been instantly at home on a horse, and surprised everyone, herself included, by becoming a neck-or-nothing rider. In two weeks she was ready to move from the placid mare of her first lessons to a more spirited animal, although not as spirited as she would have liked. The grooms despaired of controlling her before she broke her neck, and Ninian took over the task.

At first, as a precaution, he took his groom, Halton, a burly individual who was obviously devoted to his master and disliked allowing him out of his sight. Calvina found his presence strangely oppressive and was glad when Ninian declared that she no longer needed an escort of two and dispensed with Halton's company.

She loved riding over the estate with Ninian. Out-of-doors they could talk more freely, and he tried to dispel the dark rumors that swirled about his cousin. "You mustn't believe all the lurid tales you hear about Rupert. I've known him all my life, and I've seen how kind he can be."

"I imagine he could be kind to those he loved," Calvina murmured, almost to herself.

"Indeed he can. He's gentleness itself to Aunt Josie. And look how he came to your rescue on the street that night."

"He did that because it provided him with 'entertainment.' He told me so."

"Oh, he likes to talk like that. It means nothing."

"But if you could have seen his face as he dealt with those men. It was almost inhuman."

"I won't deny he has a temper, and when his black moods are on him there's no knowing what he'll do. There was a stupid boy once who challenged him to a duel over a trifle. It was madness, because Rupert can put a bullet through a man's heart at a hundred paces."

Calvina gasped. "He's really done such a thing?"

"So they say. I didn't see it myself, but there are men who swear they did. The thing is, he shouldn't have accepted the challenge. The lad was tipsy and if Rupert had shrugged it off no one would have thought the worse of him. But he was mad with pride and rage, and he insisted on going through with it."

"You mean he killed him?" Calvina asked, horrified.

"No. Luckily someone alerted the magistrates and it was called off. The boy very sensibly vanished."

"Thank heavens! Who informed the magistrates?"

"Nobody knows," Ninian said quickly. "Whoever it was was wise enough not to let Rupert find out."

He refused to meet her eyes, and the conviction grew on her that it was Ninian himself who'd informed. But he declined to speak further on this matter, a reticence for which she honored him and which further convinced her that her suspicions were correct. The next moment he'd spurred his horse, challenging her to keep up. In racing after him she forgot everything except that she was enjoying life as never before.

Chapter Four

At last the White Room was ready for Calvina. Initially she was a little daunted by its splendor. It was dominated by a huge four-poster bed, hung with rich velvet curtains. Everywhere were the colors of autumn: light and dark browns, fawn, orange, pale yellow.

"But why is it called the White Room?" she asked.

"Because my brother, Rupert's father, was an evil man," Aunt Josie replied seriously. "They said he was the worst blackguard for miles about. His wife was a gentle soul, as good as he was bad. Despite everything, she loved him, and his unkindness broke her heart. Near the end of her life she barely left this room. It was known as the White Room, as his was known as the Black. I loved her dearly. Sometimes I think she's still here. But never let that thought trouble you. There was only loving kindness in her."

They went to view the portraits of Rupert's parents in the gallery. Lord Thomas Glennister's pose—standing at a window, books to one side of him, rolling acres to the other—implied a great man, at ease with learning and agriculture. But the painter had been too honest to hide the truth. The dark eyes were mean, grasping, full of cold selfishness, and perhaps something even more horrible.

Araminta, his wife, had a sensitive, melancholy face. The sweet lips seemed about to smile as she gazed at the little boy beside her. Certainly Rupert had been a beautiful child, Calvina thought. His face then hadn't developed the look of derision.

Once she'd grown used to the finery of her bedroom she was comfortable there. As Aunt Josie had said, Araminta's sweet soul seemed to linger.

Sometimes she would lie in the darkness and think about Toby. Had he heard of her marriage, and if so, did he think she'd forgotten him? If only there was some way to tell him that he would always be her true love. When she fell asleep her pillow would often be wet with tears.

Her days were filled with preparations for her new life: lessons in music, dancing, etiquette, food, and wine. Calvina and her father had eaten good plain fare, and the food at the Dalrymples had combined pretension with bad cooking. The cook at Glennister Court revealed to her the secrets of oyster loaves, sole in red wine, and ragout of cucumber, and Aunt Josie taught her how to choose the menu for a grand dinner party.

The evenings were spent on something Josie called "familiarity with the polite world" which turned out to be gossip about scandals old and new. They were called criminal connections, "crim cons" for short, and although a society lady should maintain a discreet silence in public, it was helpful to know which of Lady X's children had not been fathered by Lord X.

"But only the younger children," Aunt Josie said comfortably. "Naturally there's no question of such a thing until she has presented her husband with a son, and preferably two."

"Indeed, ma'am," Calvina said, her head spinning.

Aunt Josie loved to gossip, and once started she grew carried away and revealed more than she intended. Calvina gathered that the Glennister face could be found in society with unseemly frequency.

In her rare moments to herself Calvina would look over the house. She found it poorly lit and as sullen as her first impression. It had never been a happy home, and it wasn't one now, despite Josie's best endeavors.

Very early one morning she went to explore the end of the building that had once been the castle. It was very quiet in this part, as though people avoided it. Most of the doors were locked, but at last she came to one at the far end of a corridor, whose handle turned easily. On the threshold she stopped, dumbfounded by what met her eyes.

The room was a kind of laboratory, full of chemicals, retorts, strange smells, and peculiar-looking instruments. A huge window dominated one side of it, and in its light stood a large desk. Zodiac charts lay on the desk, and a book lay open at an elaborate diagram. If Lord Rupert Glennister had wanted to confirm his mysterious reputation this was just the room to do it.

Calvina studied the papers on the desk. Many of them contained chemical formulae, and these put her at ease, for she was used to making up medicines for the poor. She recognized many of the chemicals and herbs mentioned and was beginning to relax when she was startled by a hissing sound from behind a curtain she hadn't previously noticed.

Drawing it back slightly she saw a small alcove. Rupert was standing at a table covered in glass pipes and retorts, concentrating on pouring a violently colored liquid from one container into another. He was almost in darkness, lit only by a candle, which threw its dancing yellow light onto his face. Steam rose as the liquid bubbled and boiled, and she could almost believe him to be looming up from hell.

"Either come in or go out, but drop that curtain before the light ruins what I'm doing."

His voice, exasperated and very human, broke the spell. She stepped in and pulled the curtain behind her. He'd spoken without glancing up. Nor did he look at her now. All his attention was for his task. Calvina put a handkerchief over her mouth against the dreadful smell.

"This place isn't for those with weak stomachs," he agreed with a satirical grin.

"What—what is that you're making?" She choked.

"Poison, of course, to dispose of my enemies. I'm

61

surprised you felt the need to ask. Well, is everything as you expected?"

"I'm not sure what I expected," she replied cautiously.

"Demons and spells, satanic incantations, perhaps a Black Mass or two and the odd human sacrifice?"

She laughed at the absurdity, and at last he glanced up, approval in his eyes. It was the first time they'd seen each other since their strange marriage, more than a month ago. Rupert was in his shirtsleeves and looked as if he'd been here some time.

"All right, I've finished. Let's get away from the smell." He ushered her through the curtain, dropping it again behind them.

"I didn't know you'd returned," she said.

"I arrived last night when the house was asleep and came straight here to work. There were some experiments that I didn't want to delay. You'll forgive my not flying to my bride directly, full of ardor."

"That would have been very disagreeable," she retorted.

His eyes flashed. "Very good, Calvina. I wondered how long it would be before you discovered my laboratory. What do you think?" He flung out an arm, indicating the whole room. "Is it wicked enough?"

In the dawn light his reputation seemed mere foolishness, and she answered eagerly, "My father knew an astronomer who had charts like these. I found them wonderful." She leaned over them. "When he talked about the stars he made me feel part of a mighty world." She hesitated.

"Go on," he said, watching her keenly.

She needed no further encouragement. Once she'd started to talk the thoughts spilled out. A few she'd learned from the astronomer who'd taught her. But the questions were her own, and it was bliss to find that Rupert could answer them. Better still was the fact that he spoke seriously, not seeming shocked at her interest in matters outside a woman's sphere. Somehow the time slipped away.

"Goodness, we've been talking for nearly an hour!" she exclaimed.

His eyes held an odd, arrested look. "And not one moment of boredom," he said, almost to himself. "What is it? Why did you make that face? Did I bore you after all? Was this nothing but a performance called, 'being a dutiful wife'?"

"Oh no," she said hastily. "I've never been so fascinated in my life. It's just that I suddenly thought of Hugh Dalrymple. He would get angry if I spoke like this. He said a display of unwomanly knowledge was a mark of pride."

"Forget him. You're out of his clutches now. You can say what you like to me. I prefer a woman with something in her head beyond frills and furbelows."

Calvina laughed. "My knowledge of frills and furbelows is sadly deficient. Aunt Josie was shocked to discover that I didn't know the difference between bombazine and Berlin silk."

"But you're improving daily, I hear. In every letter she says how pleased she is with you."

Calvina stared. "You and she have been corresponding about me?"

"Of course." He saw her odd look and asked impatiently, "Is there a reason why I shouldn't write to my own aunt?"

"No, but you might have written to me, too."

"Whatever for?"

"Because, unless I imagined it, we went through a marriage ceremony some weeks back," Calvina said indignantly.

He shrugged. "So we did. But I warned you I wouldn't be the sort of husband who sat in your pocket."

"I shouldn't want that either, but surely a note to ask if I was happy . . . or at least comfortable . . ."

"But I know you can't be happy because you'll be

grieving over that other fellow . . . I expect you remember his name better than I do. And I asked my aunt to make sure you were comfortable. So that seems to take care of everything."

Calvina seethed, beyond speech.

"By the way," Lord Rupert added, as if recalling a minor detail, "you must forgive a husband's vulgar curiosity, but has he written you any billets-doux, pledges of undying love, that sort of thing?"

"Certainly not. We have renounced each other."

He raised a cynical eyebrow. "Not a word, a note, a pebble at your window?"

"You have my word of honor that Toby has made no attempt to contact me."

"Good grief. What a cawker! I shall have to meet this paragon of dreary virtue, invite him for a night's drinking, see if I can't put some life into him."

"No," Calvina said furiously. "I forbid you to do any such thing."

"Forbid?" he echoed, amused. "Dear wife, do you think you can forbid me, or that I would take the slightest notice of you?"

"But you mustn't speak to him. Please."

"Never fear. I shan't put a bullet through him. Or perhaps you're worried that he might put one through me. Should I be in a quake? You know him better than I do."

Calvina tightened her lips and turned away, but he only laughed and pulled her around to face him, holding her there with his hands on her shoulders. She could feel his warmth through her dress, and it brought back shocking memories that she'd thought had faded. It was unnerving to stand so close to him, but even more unnerving was the glint in his eyes that was part laughter and part something else.

"A definite improvement," he said, indicating her morning dress of honey-colored sarcenet with a touch of embroidery at the throat. "Anything is better than those black and gray abominations you wore before. My compliments."

"Aunt Josie helped me choose the material . . ." she began, pleased by his approval.

"Yes, I told her that color would suit you," he said carelessly.

Calvina took a deep breath, her indignation rising again. "Did you indeed, my lord? No doubt you also advised her how much embroidery should go on my chemise."

"My dear ma'am, you put me to the blush. In polite society, I must inform you, a lady doesn't discuss her—er—chemise, especially with a gentleman she barely knows."

Calvina's cheeks flamed. "I must have been mad to marry you."

"We were both a little mad that night," he said, a strange look in his eyes. "You were desperate and I—well, it's done now."

"You mean you have regrets?"

"I never regret any action of mine," he said harshly. "I can't afford to. I turn every situation to my account, as I'll teach you to do."

But then, like lightning, his mood changed. His black look faded as if it had never been, and he took her hands, smiling into her eyes with more warmth than she'd seen in him before. "Don't be angry with me, especially when I'm so pleased with you."

"Are you really?" she asked with a touch of shyness.

"Yes. You'll serve my purpose splendidly."

He released her hands as he spoke and so didn't see the faint look of disappointment on her face at this prosaic way of putting things.

"It took a lot of spirit to come investigating this part of the house," he said. "Let's test your courage a little further."

Abruptly he pulled back a curtain revealing a large painting on the wall. It was another portrait of Lord

Thomas, but unlike the sedate likeness in the gallery, this one was surrounded by the heads of snarling demons and the trappings of a wizard.

"They called my father the devil, and his son a limb of Satan," Rupert said, regarding the picture. "He cared nothing for their opinions, nor do I. So tell me, do *you* think I'm a limb of Satan?"

"I think you'd like me to believe you are," Calvina replied. "But you'll need to try much harder before I'm impressed."

"Well done, my dear." He grinned. "Your father would be proud of you for that answer, and for bearding the lion in his den."

"How do you know that?"

"Because he believed that sin should be confronted and fought to the death."

"Yes, he said so in one of his books," Calvina agreed. "But how do you come to have read it?"

He shrugged. "No doubt I picked it up somewhere. I have an extensive library."

"Papa's works aren't in your library," Calvina said, her curiosity growing.

"Nonsense. Ninian reads them."

"Yes, but they're his own copies, kept in his own rooms. He told me." Her lips twitched. "Admit it. You bought one."

He regarded her with chagrin. "Very well. It seemed advisable to study the mind of the man who raised you. And if you laugh at me I shall turn you into a spotted toad."

But his own eyes were gleaming with something that might have been amusement, and even respect.

"What did you read?" she asked, dutifully preserving a straight face.

He named two of her father's longer and more difficult works, and she stared. "Every word?"

"Your amazement is unflattering, ma'am. Let me inform you that I not only read every word, I understood every word. Having done so, I can only be glad that my late father-in-law wasn't a Calvinist in the strictest sense of the term."

"He didn't believe in predestination," she agreed, correctly interpreting this.

"Mind you, it was a doctrine that appealed to me when I was a very young man," Rupert confessed. "The notion that I was destined for hell from the moment of my birth seemed both amusing and romantic, besides relieving me of all responsibility."

"But how dull," she said lightly. "Where is the fun in being a great sinner if you can't take any of the credit for it?"

"By God, you *are* laughing at me!"

"I assure you, I wouldn't dare," she said with a touch of impishness. "How fortunate for you that no one believes in predestination anymore—"

"And I can go to perdition in my own way," he completed. After a moment they shared a laugh.

He put away his papers and shrugged on his coat, saying, "I will admit that your father surprised me by the generosity of his Calvinism."

"No one who'd met him would be surprised by his generosity," Calvina said at once. "Or by his gentleness, or his loving kindness. His own life was austere, but his heart reached out to everyone. He said that no sin was so black that it couldn't be reached by love."

Rupert frowned and eyed her somewhat askance. "Do you, by any chance, harbor hopes of reforming me?"

"Certainly not. Your salvation is in your hands, not mine."

"Shouldn't a good wife try to reclaim her husband's soul?"

She regarded him steadily. "I would think it an act of grave impertinence to meddle with your soul," she said truthfully.

She could see he was taken aback. After a long moment, during which he seemed to be recovering his poise, he said coolly, "What an unexpected woman you are! You once told me you're not given to the vapors and I see it's true, for which I give thanks to whichever master you believe I serve."

"Perhaps you think—" she began, but he interrupted her.

"I think only that we should present ourselves for breakfast. My aunt will scold us if we're late."

He was ushering her out as he spoke, and it was clear that the brief mental spark that had flashed between them was something he didn't wish to pursue. She guessed that if she'd shown any tendency to preach or interfere he would instantly have given her a set down. By throwing him back on himself she'd made him strangely uneasy.

She was sure of it a moment later when he said casually, "We won't meet again until this evening. I have much business to see to on the estate. I doubt I'll even return for dinner. But perhaps you'll be so good as to be in the library at ten o'clock. I should be home by then, and will hope not to keep you waiting too long."

Before she could answer he turned abruptly aside and vanished down another corridor, leaving Calvina staring after him, wondering about the man she'd married.

At the appointed hour that evening she went to the library, but she could see no sign of Rupert. Her attention was taken by a table, lit by three six-branched candelabra. Their flickering lights fell on a huge collection of jewels laid out underneath. There were necklaces, tiaras, brooches, earrings, and bracelets, made of gold and silver, studded with jewels. She hadn't known there were such gems in the world: rubies, emeralds, sapphires, and diamonds. She regarded them curiously. So this was what people meant by a king's ransom!

Rupert rose from a chair by the fire. "It was time I presented you with the family jewels," he said. "Some of them are old-fashioned and will need resetting, but you can decide that later."

"Yes, indeed." She was too bemused to think of anything else to say.

"I hope you feel that I'm keeping my side of the bargain."

"And I shall keep mine, of course." She continued to look at the display, overwhelmed and uneasy.

"It's considered polite to show some interest when your husband bestows a fortune on you," Rupert said sardonically.

"Forgive me. They are magnificent. It's only . . ."

"Too worldly for you? You'll have to learn to be a little worldly if you're to maintain your position as my wife."

"I'll do my best. It's just that I couldn't help thinking for a moment of my little pearl brooch that the Dalrymples stole."

"I recall it. A trifle. Does it mean more to you than all these?"

"It's all I had of my mother," Calvina said wistfully. "I was very young when she died, and I hardly remember her. But Papa gave it to me when I was fourteen. It had belonged to his own mother and he gave it to Mama on their wedding day. She wore it all her life, and he only took it from her when she died. He wept as he told me that. Since I lost him, I've sometimes looked at it and felt closer to them both."

Rupert said nothing, and Calvina saw a look on his face that seemed like boredom. What had possessed her to tell her secrets to this man? To her relief Aunt Josie appeared, exclaiming over the jewels, and the moment passed.

The announcement in *The Times* had said only that the wedding had taken place between Lord Rupert Glennister and Miss Calvina Bracewell, daughter of the Reverend Calvin Bracewell and cousin to Lord Stoneham. The marriage had been quiet owing to the recent decease of the bride's father.

These few lines caused a sensation in the polite world. Men roared with laughter. Wives pursed their lips. Young maidens wept. Lively young bucks took an extra brandy to cushion the shock.

But nowhere was the uproar greater than in the house of the Dalrymples. At Hugh's command they all dropped to their knees and prayed noisily and spitefully. But all the invocations in the world wouldn't change the fact that Calvina had married a vast fortune.

"She'll rue the day she renounced her benefactors," Hugh predicted. "Woe to she who unites herself with the beast! Scorned shall she be, even as he is scorned. Yea, they shall both be cast out!"

"But she'll be cast out in satin and diamonds," Eglantine wailed.

"What are diamonds against a peaceful soul?"

"Oh, don't be such a fool!" his wife snapped.

Eglantine suffered most. Her triumph in carrying off Toby Aylesbury had been turned to ashes beside Calvina's coup. She had a bout of hysterics and consoled herself with spending more than ever on her wedding finery. Her bridal gown was an astonishing creation of satin, lavishly adorned with lace and rosettes. With Toby chained by his promise, she was already growing lazy about her appearance and stuffed herself so greedily that the dress had to be let out twice.

She was parading in it for her misty-eyed mama when they heard a commotion downstairs and hurried out onto the landing. James had opened the front door to Lord Rupert, who strode in and demanded Hugh. On learning that he was in the room grandly called "the master's study" Rupert advanced on the door and threw it open. To the disappointment of everyone in the house he then closed it firmly.

Hugh rose from the desk where he'd been penning an improving work about the folly of worldly marriages. Something in Lord Rupert's face made him gulp, but he tried to assume the proper air. "I don't know what

70

you mean by coming here, sir, but your presence is unwelcome . . ."

"You've doubtless heard of my marriage to Miss Bracewell." Rupert threw aside his cloak but kept his malacca cane in his hand. "Don't bother refusing me your blessing because I'll do very well without it. I'm here to claim my wife's fortune."

"Fortune? What fortune?" Hugh spluttered. "She was a penniless orphan that I took in out of charity."

"She had a pearl brooch from her mother, which you stole," Rupert said coldly. "It is mine in law and I demand it."

"No such thing. She's lying. What should a baggage like that do with pearls? You've married a madwoman . . ."

"I won't bandy words with you. I give you three seconds to produce my property."

"And I tell you I don't know what you're talking about."

"In that case, you leave me no choice." Rupert turned the key in the lock. "That's better. We don't want to be disturbed by servants."

"What—what do you mean by that?" Hugh yammered.

"This," Rupert said. Moving swiftly, he seized Hugh, thrust him forward across the desk, and brought the cane down three times on his plump backside. His victim's roars brought the entire household down into the hall outside.

"Now," Rupert said, allowing him up, "my property, if you please."

"I'll have the law on you," Hugh raged.

A grin broke across Rupert's harsh face. "I don't think you will."

Hugh blanched at the prospect of describing this scene to a magistrate. Meeting perfect comprehension in Rupert's eyes he edged away to the door and turned the key with trembling hands.

"Eglantine!"

71

"I'm here, Pa." She bounced forward, still in her bridal gown.

"Take that thing off," he snapped, pointing to the brooch pinned to the dress. "Calvina wants it back."

"No! She can't have it."

"Take it off!" he screamed, keeping a wary eye on Rupert, who was watching the scene with an expression of unholy delight.

Eglantine began to howl, which made her face swell and grow bright red. Hugh seized her and removed the brooch by force, which made her howl louder. Toby arrived at that moment and regarded his betrothed with a ghastly eye.

"Take it and get out," Hugh gibbered, holding out the brooch.

Rupert pocketed it and glided out past Toby. "If you are the saintly Toby I should offer you my commiserations," he murmured. "But I fear no words would be adequate."

Calvina's maid, Sukey, wasn't a sophisticated dresser, such as Aunt Josie assured her she would need in London, but a buxom country lass, who knew how to clean clothes and keep them in good order. She was standing behind her mistress now, brushing her long fair hair before she retired for the night.

The plain nightdress was gone, replaced by one of silk, over which she wore a peignoir of lace, trimmed with satin ribbons. She looked every inch Lady Rupert Glennister, but inside she was still Calvina Bracewell, wondering what further upheavals the world held for her.

In the candlelight neither of the two women saw Rupert enter the bedroom without knocking and stand in the shadows, watching. At last Calvina rose, ready to retire. Then she heard Sukey gasp, "My lord!"

Calvina glanced up quickly and saw Rupert. He dismissed the maid with a nod and came closer, regarding her with a disturbing glint in his eyes. "Forgive me for intruding on you, but I have a gift I felt you'd wish to have at once."

At the sight of her brooch Calvina gasped in joyful disbelief. "You got it back for me. Oh, wonderful! Thank you so much. If only you knew what . . . thank you, *thank you!*"

The next moment, forgetting all else but her joy, she threw her arms about Rupert's neck, hugging him fiercely in an ecstasy of gratitude. She quickly recollected herself and tried to back off, but his arm was tight around her waist, pressing her body against the hard length of his. Breathlessly she looked up into his face and found him regarding her with one eyebrow raised in cynical amusement.

"Is that all I get?" he asked softly.

"You promised—just at first—" She could hardly speak for the thumping of her heart.

"I would make no demands on you. That was before you threw yourself into my arms."

"But I—I was grateful for your kindness—" she stammered.

His mouth twisted derisively. "I'm never kind, Calvina, except for my own ends." He touched her face with his free hand, caressing her cheek, then sliding his fingers into her free-flowing hair until they cupped her head. Deliberately he brushed his lips against hers.

"Your mouth is honey," he murmured. "How unwise of you to tempt me, if you didn't mean it."

"Let me go," she whispered, hardly able to breathe.

"When I'm ready."

"You promised—"

"I consider myself freed from my promise."

He covered her mouth before she could answer. His lips were teasing but insistent, silently commanding her to yield her will to his. She fought to hold on to her true inner self, the only part left that seemed to be still her own. But the dark magic was at work again, making her lips soften and part for him.

His tongue invaded her with small flickering movements that sent sensations of pleasure dancing along her nerves to every part of her body. The peignoir slipped to the floor, leaving her wearing only the thin silk nightgown that barely concealed her nakedness. She felt his hands roving over her slender body in intimate caresses that scandalized her even while she longed for them.

She found she was lying on the bed. Rupert had tossed aside his shirt, revealing broad shoulders and a taut, smooth chest. She had no idea how these things had happened. She was in a whirl of confusion and horror at herself. Whatever Rupert's strange power over her body, Toby was the man in her heart. How could she yield to her senses and be so false to their true love?

He brushed the hair away from her face with gentle fingers. "I want to know that I have all of you," he said raggedly. "Let me see your eyes."

But something he found in those grayish-blue depths made him stop. A tremor went through his powerful frame as he searched her face. Calvina met his gaze bravely, knowing that he'd seen into her heart.

"Damn you!" he said at last. "He's still there, isn't he? Why can't I find him and tear him out?"

Calvina forced herself to speak through the pounding in her veins. "Does it signify, my lord? Why should you want all of me? It wasn't in our bargain. Be content with what you have."

"Be damned to the bargain," he said with soft violence. "I want all of you, and I mean to have you." Abruptly he released her, tossing her back onto the bed. "But don't put yourself into a fret, my dear. When you come to my bed, you'll come willingly, as you came to my arms just now."

"Never," she said fiercely. "Never, do you understand?"

He gave a crooked smile. "We shall have to wait and see which one of us is right. Good night, my wife!"

* * *

74

Calvina hardly knew how to face Rupert the next morning, but when she did so, the mystery of her husband's character deepened.

She'd thought their consciousness of what had happened must lie between them, but he greeted her casually, almost indifferently. This made it easier, although she couldn't help feeling a little piqued.

Later she raised the subject of the brooch. There was something she had to know. "I can't imagine how you persuaded Hugh to give it up," she said.

"My dear girl, do you suppose I can't get the better of Hugh Dalrymple? That's practically an insult."

"Yes, but . . ." It was hard to go on, yet Calvina's rearing was strong in her. "You didn't . . . treat him as you did those men . . . that first night?"

"Well, I'll be . . . don't tell me you're sorry for him?"

"Not exactly that, but Papa said we should forgive our enemies."

"Do you feel forgiving toward Hugh?"

"No," she admitted. "Just the same . . ."

"Set your mind at rest. I didn't use my fists on him because it wasn't necessary. I used my cane. Three whacks on his fat rear made my point very nicely."

"You used your cane on his . . . ?" Disgraceful laughter was bubbling up inside her.

"He roared the place down," Rupert recalled with a grin. "It's a pity you weren't there. I think even your puritanical soul might have enjoyed it."

"Yes . . . I think I would . . ." The laughter came now in great gusts, not really like laughter at all. More like sobbing. She couldn't stop. All the shattering events of the last few weeks seemed to converge on her at once, exhausting, tragic, bitter, and wildly, uncontrollably funny.

"Calvina?" Rupert was staring at her.

"My lord, I think I'm having hysterics," she said, gasping.

"My lady, I think you are," he agreed dispassionately.

She reached out blindly and somehow found his arms about her, holding her tight. It wasn't like the other times. There was no passion now, just a rush to safety on her part, and a rocklike reassurance on his.

"Never had ... hysterics before ..." she managed to say.

"Never had to deal with them. I believe I'm supposed to throw a pitcher of water over you." He sounded doubtful. "Don't think that would do much good, though. More likely to make you worse. Better if you drink a little wine."

But when he tried to fetch it she clung to him, shaking violently. Her whole body was cold, as though she were in a state of shock, and suddenly the sobs of laughter had turned into sobs of grief. They made ugly whooping sounds, and when he pulled her hard against him she tried to stifle the noise against his shoulder. The two of them stood like that until she'd calmed down. Gradually the cold gave way to a feeling of warmth and safety, as though nothing could ever hurt her again. And this had something to do with the steely hardness of his arms and the firmness of his chest.

"Better now?" he asked, more kindly than she'd ever heard him before.

"Yes, thank you. I don't know what came over me."

"I'm surprised it didn't happen sooner, with everything you've been through."

How gentle his voice was, she thought. How easy it would be to stay here forever, safe and contented! But already he was pushing her away, to look at her.

"You'd better wash your face before Aunt Josie sees it," he observed in a tone that was nearer to his usual dispassionate speech. "Otherwise she'll think I've been ill-treating you."

"Then I shall tell her how kind you were," she said, suddenly shy.

"Good God! Tell her no such thing! Think of my reputation!"

The moment was over. It might never have been. As she moved to the door he called her name, his voice carefully indifferent.

"Yes, sir?" She looked back.

"What does that boy look like, the one who was your lover? Does he have light brown, curly hair and a womanish face?"

"You've seen him?" she asked eagerly.

"I believe so. He arrived at the Dalrymple house just when things were getting interesting. I offered him my sympathy. You'll be well revenged when he finds himself married to that harpy."

"I want no revenge on Toby," she said instantly. "It wasn't his fault. And I must make it plain to you, my lord, that he wasn't my 'lover.' I mean—we didn't—that is, he never—"

Rupert grinned, and the diabolical glint was there again, in his eyes. "My dear, there wasn't the least need for you to tell me that he 'never,' " he said softly.

Chapter Five

Toby and Eglantine were married in April, two months after Calvina's own wedding. It might have been coincidence that Rupert chose that very day for her to make her first public appearance as his wife. She doubted it, but she couldn't ask him. One morning he informed her that they were to attend a concert at the New Assembly Rooms that evening, and immediately departed.

"It's the perfect occasion," Aunt Josie said as she fussed around her, helping to put the final touches to her appearance. "You'll have to talk to people a little during the interval, but the rest of the time you'll sit and listen to the music." She added with disconcerting candor, "Most people will just want to stare at you anyway."

"I think it must be very disagreeable to be stared at," Calvina protested.

"But they'll stare even more when you go to London." She stepped back to regard her handiwork and sighed happily. "You'll outshine them all."

It was permissible for evening gowns to be cut low over the bosom, but Calvina had modestly insisted on a dress at least four inches higher than the fashion. Her hair, too, was still in its demure braids. But the glow of her beauty triumphed over these austere details.

Her dress was blue crepe over an underslip of white satin, and in her hand she carried Rupert's gift to mark the occasion. It was an Italian fan with carved ivory sticks embellished with gold and silver leaf, and spangles. She would have been delighted with it if only he'd given it to her himself, instead of sending it via Josie.

She wore sapphire and diamond earrings, and more sapphires sparkled on her wrist. But when it came to the matching necklace she rebelled. Why should Rupert have chosen today of all days, when her heart was breaking over Toby's marriage? True, he was no more lost to her than at the moment of her own wedding, but the thought of his making wedding vows to Eglantine was unbearably painful. In a mood of defiance Calvina slipped about her neck the little locket that bore his picture.

To her relief Rupert made no mention of the locket when he entered and studied her appearance. "Excellent," he declared at last. "Fashionable, yet restrained. Shall we go, my wife?"

She took his proffered arm and they went out to the carriage. As they reached Bath she reflected on the last time she'd seen these streets, running through them in terror, homeless and desperate. But she was returning a great lady, decked in satin and diamonds.

As they entered the Assembly Rooms all eyes were on the tall man in black, with his swarthy face and snapping dark eyes, and the slim, elegant woman by his side. Despite her jewels she looked as demure as a Quaker, her hand resting lightly in her lord's. A buzz of conjecture went around, and people pressed in from all the rooms, to see the devil and his bride.

Everyone wanted to meet her, and Rupert performed the introductions smoothly. Calvina responded with grave courtesy, but all the faces were alike to her. Her heart and mind were elsewhere, with Toby, wondering what he was doing at that moment.

When it was almost time for the concert to begin Rupert led her forward to the front row of seats. It was a relief not to have to bow and smile any longer, but to be able, under cover of the music, to lose herself in her own thoughts. But, to her dismay, the great soprano, Neroni, began her recital with a soaring love song about a bride and groom going triumphantly to their wedding.

How could Toby bear to embrace Eglantine as his wife? But then Calvina remembered herself responding fiercely to Rupert's kisses within a few minutes of their meeting, and she trembled with shame. If she'd held off, as a maiden should, she would never have fainted and there would have been no need for him to carry her into the house. The Dalrymples might never have met him that night, and the whole disaster could have been avoided. She had betrayed Toby and been punished for it.

She tried to put him out of her mind, but as ill luck would have it the last song was one she'd heard in Lady Jellineck's drawing room. It was a simple tune, whose words told of the dawning of love, and the blissful knowledge that love was requited. She'd glanced up and found Toby watching her intently. He'd smiled and she'd smiled back before modestly averting her head. Afterward they'd talked over the teacups, but she could recall nothing they'd said. Question and answer had already been given, and their eyes confirmed the joyous truth while their mouths uttered polite nothings. What malevolent fairy had chosen that song on the day Toby had united himself with another woman?

She thought how treacherous her marriage must have seemed to him! If only she could speak to him once more, and tell him that her heart would always be his, although their paths must lie apart.

She came out of her reverie to realize that the song had ended, and Rupert was speaking to her. "A fine song," she said hastily, "and beautifully sung."

He regarded her strangely. "I inquired whether you were tired, madam," he said in a cold voice.

"A little, yes."

"In that case, I think we've stayed long enough."

She departed with her head up, her hand tucked in his arm. He was silent on the way home, watching her from the other side of the carriage. Calvina couldn't see him in the darkness, but now and then she caught the gleam of his eyes and wondered if he was angry with her. It was impossible to tell from his calm demeanor.

This was what Lord Rupert intended. His dignity didn't permit him to reveal to his wife that her conduct had left him angry and baffled. His experience of women was that they either laid themselves out to please him or fled in horror. But Calvina had simply forgotten him. She'd sat in a dream as the song ended, and for an incredible moment he'd seen the glint of tears on her eyelashes. He'd understood, and his lips had tightened in displeasure. But she hadn't noticed that either.

At home he bid her good night with a curt nod.

"Rupert," she said as he turned away.

He looked back. "There is something you wish to say to me, madam?"

His cold eyes daunted her. "Nothing," she said.

He gave a small bow and left her.

Although it was spring there was a chill in the night air. After what Calvina had endured in her unheated attic at the Dalrymples', it was pleasant to undress in a bedchamber warmed by a fire.

Sukey's chatter was almost a relief. She exclaimed over her mistress's beauty, asked about the evening, and babbled on without waiting for an answer. Calvina responded mechanically. Rupert's manner had disturbed her with its undercurrent of rage held in check. She wondered if she'd done something wrong, but her only crime had been to dream of another man while in her husband's company, and he couldn't have known about that, unless . . .

She drew a sharp breath. Unless he'd read her heart by black magic. At once she chided herself for such fantasies, but the more she saw of Rupert the greater mystery he became. When the dark look came over his face she could believe him capable of anything. Anything at all.

Sukey undid Calvina's hair, letting it fall about her shoulders in waves, and taking up the brush.

"Leave me now," Calvina said suddenly. "I'll brush my own hair. Good night."

When the door had closed behind the maid she went to sit by the fire, gazing into it pensively as she drew the brush through her long tresses. The room was almost in darkness, save for a three-branched candelabra on her dressing table, and the soft glow of the coals that illuminated her face. Now at last she could be alone with her dreams of Toby. As well as sadness there were happier memories, such as the moment when they'd exchanged vows of love, and the look in his eyes as he gave her the locket. She touched it, hidden beneath her silk nightdress that buttoned modestly up to the throat.

She didn't know that she was smiling, but the man watching her saw it. He'd entered the room as Sukey left and stood in the shadows, regarding his wife with a puzzled frown. He was ill at ease, a feeling that puzzled and angered him. Everything had seemed simple on the night of their wedding. Calvina would serve his purpose, and she pleased him physically. Later he'd discovered that she was also intelligent. What more could he want? Her difference from other women made her ideal.

But now he was discovering that that very difference held another element, one that might thwart him. And he wasn't used to being thwarted. The mysterious smile that touched her lips in the firelight made him realize, with a jolt, that she kept her thoughts a secret.

Something in the silence made her look up. The sight of Rupert startled her. He'd stripped off his shirt, and now wore only breeches and a red-silk dressing gown. It hung open at the front, revealing his broad, muscular chest, with its light covering of hair. Calvina wondered how long he'd been there. He was very still, and although the candlelight fell on his face his eyes were in shadow.

"Rupert . . ." she said uncertainly.

"You were not expecting me, madam?"

"No."

"Perhaps you should have been."

A little pulse began to beat in her throat at a certain note in his voice.

"You did well tonight," he went on. "Everyone admired you, including your husband."

"Thank you. I'm glad you felt I did you credit."

"It was more than that. I don't think I realized before how beautiful you are."

He took the brush from her and set it aside, drawing her to her feet. With gentle fingers he brushed back the hair from her face, watching her features intently. But when he tried to hold her more closely, she stiffened.

"Rupert . . . you promised . . . at least for a while . . ."

"It's been a long enough while," he growled. As he spoke he rained kisses over her neck and throat, and Calvina felt the familiar warmth steal over her body. She almost cried out her dismay. How could he cast his black enchantment over her at this moment, when her heart was possessed by love for Toby?

Suddenly she felt him grow still and tense. There was a black look in his eyes as they fell on the locket about her neck. "What's this?" he demanded, taking it between his fingers. "I've covered you with jewels. Why do you wear this cheap trumpery thing?"

She tried to snatch it away, but his fingers were like steel, keeping hold of the locket and prying it open. As he saw Toby's picture his expression grew ugly. "My wife does not wear the picture of another man," he said dangerously. "Do I have to tell you that?"

"How can you call me your wife?" she demanded. "Our marriage is a mockery."

"You're my wife, and you'll behave with perfect propriety. Otherwise you're no use to me. How dare you carry this man against your heart in public!"

"I love him," she cried. "And he loves me."

"Ah yes," Rupert said derisively. "He loves you so

much that today he let himself be forced to the altar with another woman."

"You knew it was today?" she cried in accusation.

"I've made it my business to know, and the more I've discovered the more I've been astonished at your wasting a moment on him. Why did this fine hero let himself be marched off like a lamb to the slaughter? Why hasn't he been here, beating down the doors to protect you? By God, before I saw the woman I loved wed a man of my reputation I'd call him out."

"Toby is fine and noble—"

"And I'm a very good shot," he jeered.

"If you think he's afraid of you—"

"If he isn't he's a fool."

"Well, I'm not afraid of you, and I'm telling you to get out of my room."

He released her. He was smiling, but his smile was more disturbing than his rage. "Very good, Calvina. Very brave. But aren't you just a little scared of me? I might change you into a mouse or turn your hair white by evil incantations."

"Silly stories to scare children!" she said firmly. "I don't believe a word of it."

A gleam of admiration came into his eyes. "I think you really mean that."

"I do. And I also mean it when I tell you to leave."

"It's been twenty years or more since I obeyed an order from anyone, man or woman. But I'll leave you because I don't care to sleep three in a bed."

"No, *four* in a bed is more your style," she snapped, remembering what she'd seen in his lodgings that first night.

He didn't bother asking what she meant. "You're learning," he said. "But don't learn too fast. I want the pleasure of teaching you slowly. On the night that I claim you there'll be no Toby Aylesbury in your head or your heart, and by morning you'll have forgotten he ever existed."

"Never," Calvina said quietly. "I shall love him all my life. Let this matter be, my lord. It's something you'll never understand."

That drove him to madness. He seized the locket, jerked it from her neck, and tossed it in the direction of the fire. Calvina gave a cry and rushed over, dropping to her knees. "No," she screamed, clawing at the coals.

Luckily the fire had burned down. She winced as she touched the coals, and blew on her fingers. Absorbed, she didn't notice her husband watching her, or the grim look on his face as she opened the locket and wet Toby's picture with her tears. She only heard the door slam behind him and gave thanks that he was gone.

The following day he announced that it was time they left for London, and by the end of the week they were installed in Glennister House in London's Berkeley Square.

Over breakfast on their second morning in London Rupert said, "Did your father ever take you to the opera?"

"We heard some oratorios together, but Papa considered opera frivolous."

"Then you'll enjoy your first visit to Covent Garden."

"When?" Calvina asked eagerly.

"Tonight. Your debut shouldn't be delayed."

He said no more but Calvina knew what was expected of her. When the evening came she attired herself in gray silk, shot through with pink, cut high over the bosom, and decorated with blond lace. A pearl necklace and earrings were her only jewels, and her hair was dressed in its usual neat braids. More pearls studded her gray-velvet cloak, with its lining of satin.

Rupert surveyed her critically before saying, "Exactly right." By which she understood that she looked sufficiently virtuous to astonish society.

She was entranced at the sight of the great opera house with its seats going up to the roof, and tiers of boxes lining the sides. As Lord Rupert was a lover of music he rented a box on the lowest, most costly tier. It was large enough to receive visitors or to partake of a light supper in the interval.

Interested eyes flickered their way from the moment he led his wife to the front of the box and assisted her with her cloak. Knowing what was expected of her, Calvina allowed time for everyone to see her properly.

A man came to their box. He was in his late thirties, slightly built, exquisitely dressed, and everything about him was perfect. Rupert rose quickly, exclaiming, "Simmington," in a pleased voice.

Alaric Simmington had no title, but he had somehow established himself as the arbiter of taste. He was the picture of elegance down to the last detail of his snowy cravat, in which nestled a flawless diamond, and his dark blue-satin coat and matching knee breeches. He greeted Calvina with a charming bow and a smile that concealed the fact that he was inspecting her minutely. What he saw seemed to satisfy him for his eyes grew warmer and sparkled with ironic amusement.

The opera was Mozart's *The Marriage of Figaro*, and Calvina sat through it entranced. The stately oratorios she'd heard had been nothing like this colorful, enchanting work. She kept her eyes fixed on the stage, her hands clasped to her breast in wonder, and never saw the opera glasses trained on her from all over the house, or the raised eyebrows behind them.

In the first interval a haughty-looking woman made a majestic appearance in their box. She was past her first youth, with a shrewish face that still bore traces of beauty. She had dark hair and dark eyes that snapped as they looked at Calvina. Rupert greeted her as Sally, and introduced her as Lady Allbright.

"My dear, you were the sensation of London before anyone saw you," the newcomer purred to her. "Who would have thought of Rupert making an impulsive love match? You must tell me how it all came about." Her eyes gleamed with malice.

"Don't be vulgar, Sally," Rupert said amiably.

"I swear I'm the soul of amiability," Sally Allbright declared with a bright laugh. "I shall give a party for you both, and you must also come to the ball we're giving to celebrate Julia's engagement. Julia is my eldest daughter, you know," she confided to Calvina. "Some people say that I don't look old enough to have a daughter of seventeen, let alone a son of twenty-four, but when a woman's married it's time to give up thinking of her own looks, don't you think? Well, I can tell that you do."

"Nobody could think my wife's appearance anything but perfect," Rupert said in a voice that held a warning. "Let me fetch you some champagne. Simmington will look after Calvina for a moment."

Simmington, who'd just reappeared, made a small bow while Rupert steered Lady Allbright firmly out of the box.

"Flex your claws on me, Sally," he told her coolly. "It don't bother me, but I won't have my wife upset."

"My dear, how gallant!"

"Understand me. I don't want to hear her name on your lips."

"Of course. Why should we ever mention her? You're back. That's the important thing. Lysandra Ullaston's out of town, you know. That old bore she married insisted on visiting his family seat and making her do the pretty to all the rustics. She'll be furious that I saw you first."

"Lady Ullaston is another subject on which I prefer you to stay silent. Watch your tongue, Sally. It'll get you into trouble one day."

A chill went up her spine at a hint of menace in his eyes. There had always been something frightening in Rupert's ability to change from light to darkness in an instant. It was part of the thrill of knowing him, but sometimes he unnerved her. "You will accept my invitations, won't you?" she asked, recovering.

"Naturally. How delightful to know that I'm welcome again!"

"You were always welcome . . . in my heart."

"In your what?" he asked, grinning.

"Oh, confound you! Why should we talk insipid commonplaces? You have something very special to give a woman, Rupert, and I've missed it damnably."

"Aren't you forgetting that I'm a respectable married man now?"

"Respectable? You? I swear your marriage is the best joke you've ever played on society. When I threw you out I never dreamed you'd go to these lengths to get back. It's the greatest compliment any man's ever paid me."

"You flatter yourself."

She gave a coarse laugh. "No, I don't, darling. I know there are other mares in the paddock, but they can wait their turn. And don't worry. I'll be discretion itself. We'll keep your little wife happy, and she can continue playing her part. She's charming, charming!"

She tripped away. Rupert's eyes, as they gazed after her, held an unreadable expression.

Returning to his box he found Countess Lieven, one of the patronesses of Almack's, sitting with his wife. She was a coldly haughty woman, but she seemed to approve of her new acquaintance. Calvina was gravely courteous, but she neither simpered nor seemed overawed. She was unaware that this was one of the most socially powerful women in London, and if she had known, her manner would not have altered.

"You dog!" Simmington murmured to Rupert. "If you don't set the ton on its ears in one way you contrive to do it in another." He rubbed his hands. "I can see that I'm going to make a great many calls tomorrow. Don't worry. She'll take. Never fear!"

"Do you imagine my wife needs your countenance to be a success?" Rupert demanded coolly.

"No, my dear fellow. But she'll be a great deal more comfortable if she has it."

Simmington spoke no more than the truth. The news that he was impressed with the new bride was all over London the following day. Everyone in the polite world knew what had caused Lord Rupert to storm off in a rage. The announcement of his marriage to a daughter of the clergy had been greeted with disbelief and astonishment. Many of them had heard of the Reverend Calvin Bracewell. Some had heard him preach at Oxford. One elderly lady had even met him and his daughter.

"That was years ago," Lady Wilmington recalled. "He was bringing that gel up to be as big a puritan as himself. So she was induced to marry Devil Glennister, eh?"

"I wonder how much he offered her," the present Lord Wilmington mused. "He was always full of juice."

"Don't be a bigger fool than you can help," his mother adjured him caustically. "Bracewell's daughter never married for money. It must be something else. Perhaps she thinks she's going to reclaim his soul." She went off into a cackle. "I must call on her."

She did so, arriving in Berkeley Square in state one morning. A chaise and four, with the Wilmington crest on the panels, drew up and disgorged a small, thin woman dressed in the fashion of twenty years ago. Despite this no one would have dismissed her as a mere dowdy. Her son had been heard to complain that her extravagance left him with empty pockets.

Calvina received her visitor without agitation, and even remembered their one meeting.

"Interesting man, your father," Lady Wilmington recalled. "Told me to my face that I was a tough old sinner. Wonder what he said behind my back."

Calvina laughed and said truthfully, "He only told me that you had much to bear, ma'am."

"So he knew about my son, did he? Much to bear! True enough. It's a woman's fate to bear burdens, as you'll find if you haven't already. This marriage is likely to be more of a burden than you looked for."

"I have no complaints," Calvina said proudly.

"What I'd like to know is what he told you to make you do it. You needn't tell me that's none of my business, for I know that."

"I wasn't going to say any such thing, but if you think my husband offered me Spanish coin, you're quite out. He told me frankly that he wants to make the ton eat its words."

"Well, you're a plain speaker, and no mistake! I like you. You won't be short of company, because you're not in the common way. But if you ever need a true friend, come to me."

It seemed unlikely that Calvina would need such assistance. Countess Lieven sent her vouchers for Almack's, where she made a quietly successful debut. She was nervous of dancing in public for the first time, and it was a strain to remember all the stately figures of the minuet, but Rupert, looking splendidly handsome in black evening rig, was there to guide her. He was as far from being a dandy as any man could be. No fobs or seals adorned his person. A pearl in his snowy neck cloth was his only jewelry. But there was a splendor about his height, the set of his shoulders, and the natural authority that radiated from him, that outshone every man there.

The country dances held fewer terrors for Calvina. Rupert declined to take part in these, but stood by while his wife danced with Lady Allbright's eldest son, Antony. He was a pleasant, shy youth, who seemed inclined to admire the new bride rather more than was proper.

"You're already forming your own court, I see," Rupert said amiably as he led his wife to tea. "Your husband will soon be quite in the way."

"Oh, no," she said, horrified. "I never meant you to think—oh, please tell me, have I gone beyond the line?"

"Not at all. I assure you that it's quite the thing for a married woman to enjoy a circle of admirers."

"But that's not what I—I mean, why you—" Unable to think straight under his satirical eye she blurted out, "If I'm no better than the others I'm no use to you."

She could have bitten her tongue for this scandalously frank speech, but her husband let out such a crack of laughter that heads turned everywhere. Men and women looked at each other, as if wondering what Devil Glennister thought he was about, finding such entertainment in the society of a wife who was as meek as a nun's hen.

Rupert had spoken no more than the truth when he said he despised society. Having been readmitted to the ton, he shrugged and turned away. He would accompany his wife to parties, and even to Almack's, while she was still finding her feet, but once her success was assured he began to be absent for days on end.

True to their agreement, Calvina asked him no questions, but she found herself disturbingly aware of his comings and goings, and consumed with curiosity. When she learned that Glennister House had been reopened on his marriage, after being empty for years, she decided he must have another residence in which to indulge his pleasures, as in Bath.

Her suspicions were at last confirmed by an indiscretion of the Hadden twins. These two young men were twenty-five years old, like as two peas, with lean, handsome faces and, as Lady Wilmington caustically observed, more charm than was good for them. Simon the elder was heir to an earldom. George, thirty minutes his junior, had to look forward to merely a younger brother's portion. But their mutual attachment was strong. They dressed alike, thought alike, enjoyed drinking and the more vulgar sports together, and fell in love with the same women. Since they shared an aversion to respectable domestic life few of their loves were single, and the rest were ineligible for reasons too delicate to be spoken in polite company.

They were not Calvina's only cicisbeos, but they were

the most constant and attentive. Simon taught her to drive a phaeton and four, while George always claimed the first dance with her at Almack's and entertained her with the latest scandal. It was George, more thoughtless and quick of tongue than his brother, who let out the secret.

The three of them were sitting out a dance together. The twins had found a small sofa by the wall, and seated themselves one on each side of her. Calvina had been worrying lest Rupert should fail to return in time for Lady Ullaston's party. "For it's tomorrow and there's no sign of him."

"Well, he ain't gone far," George observed. "I was sparring with him in Jackson's Saloon this morning. Thought I'd pop one in over his guard. Didn't manage it, of course. He was most anxious to know that Simon and I were attending to your comfort. Said we'd have him to deal with if we weren't."

"I'll give him a report full of praise when he returns," Calvina replied gaily. "As long as he's gone no further than his lodgings I have nothing to worry about."

There was a small silence, in which George finally became aware of his brother's frantic signalling for him to keep quiet. He gulped and recovered himself. "Well, if you already knew . . ." he said awkwardly.

"About his lodgings? But I didn't, dear George. Not until you just told me."

"George scowled at his brother. "It ain't no use making faces at me now," he complained. "Too late."

"It don't mean anything, Calvina," Simon said. "Plenty of fellows don't like their wives to see them when they're a bit in their cups. If they keep a set of rooms they can drink all they like without offending a lady's sensibilities."

"Of course that must be it," she said thoughtfully. "How fortunate I am to have you two to explain things to me."

"Glad to be of help," Simon murmured.

"Up to every rig," George assured her.

"Then you'll also be able to explain why people go quiet if I mention Lady Ullaston. When I told Lady Castlereagh about the party she pursed her lips and said, '*Hmmm!*' in a very significant way. Do you know why?"

"No," the twins said in one voice.

"Oh dear!" Calvina sighed. "Perhaps I should ask Rupert directly. I can mention his lodgings at the same time."

"Don't do that!" they said, alarmed.

"You think he wouldn't like it?"

"*We* wouldn't like it," Simon said firmly.

"He'd want to know how you knew," George explained.

"And you'd be sure to tell him," Simon added gloomily.

"Of course. How could I refuse to answer my husband?"

"He'd fry our liver," George predicted.

"I'm afraid he would," Calvina agreed with her most charming smile.

The twins looked at each other, at her, then again at each other.

"George, we've been nursing a viper in our bosom."

"Simon, I'm afraid we have."

"It's nothing," Simon said. "Lysandra Ullaston and Rupert—well. But that was when he was single," he added hastily. "Married man now. Not the thing."

"I don't think Rupert cares about being the thing," Calvina said, a touch forlornly. "What is she like?"

"She makes me uneasy," Simon said. "What's a woman of thirty doing married to a man of seventy?"

"No mystery about that," George observed. "Ullaston's as rich as a nabob. His family hates Lysandra. He's got six children by the first wife, and they can see their inheritance being frittered away on her. Thing is, Ullaston's health is failing."

"And she thought she could make Rupert her second

93

husband?" asked Calvina, who'd learned some worldly wisdom by now.

"I told you, it's all over," Simon said, looking harassed. "Don't suppose he's seen her recently. That's probably why she's giving the party."

"Of course," Calvina said quietly. "I think I'd like to dance again now."

For the rest of the evening she wore a merry face, but inwardly she was struggling with herself. For some reason Rupert's kisses had returned to haunt her. She'd fought those treacherous memories down, but now they wouldn't be suppressed. Her husband lived a secret life in private lodgings about which she must never ask. And that life included women who wouldn't repulse him as she herself had done. Women who would melt in his arms and raise their faces to his kisses, content to drown in fierce, beautiful sensation.

Once she'd known nothing of such things, and now, with all her heart she longed to be back in that time. For then there'd been no tormenting feelings searing her body, making her forget everything but the man who could inspire them, and who wasn't here.

Chapter Six

Rupert arrived home at the last moment and sent his wife word that he was dressing for the evening and would be with her directly.

He appeared in due course, saluted her with a kiss on the cheek and asked if she were ready. He was attired in black-satin knee breeches, a white waistcoat and a coat with long tails, and appeared the pattern of propriety and elegance. No one regarding his sedate attire could have guessed the turbulence of his life.

Calvina, as usual, was quietly dressed. Her ball gown was made of very pale blue silk, trimmed with gauze, with a modestly high bosom. Around her long neck she wore a choker of sapphires, and more sapphires set off her ears. Rupert nodded his approval and assisted her with her blue satin cloak, trimmed with swansdown.

Ullaston House was in Grosvenor Square. Calvina spent the short journey inwardly preparing for the meeting with the woman everyone knew had been Rupert's mistress. And perhaps still was. She was still trying to talk herself into a rational state of mind when the carriage stopped.

The first thing to strike her about Ullaston House was its vulgarity. Everything was new. Everything was adorned with startling colors and patterns. Everything proclaimed loudly that money had been spent.

Lady Ullaston was a tall, statuesque woman, with a voluptuous build and a head of flaming red hair. What had possessed her to trick herself out in a gown of turquoise satin, adorned with black lace, sporting rubies set in gold, no one could think. But Lysandra had never been one to conceal her charms, as several gentlemen now present could have testified. The gown was scandalously low cut, revealing luscious milky white breasts, so blatant that Calvina's instinct was to avert her eyes.

She controlled the impulse, however, and the next moment wished she hadn't. It might have been better not to see Rupert bow low over Lysandra Ullaston's hand, or the way his lips brushed it.

One who appeared to see nothing was Lord Ullaston. An elderly gentleman of meek demeanor, he stood by his wife's side, ignored by her. He looked weary, as though he would rather be anywhere else, but now and then his eyes strayed toward her with a mixture of admiration and alarm.

"It's such a pleasure to meet the woman all London is talking about," Lysandra gushed to Calvina. "I've put you between Lord Sidelman, *such* an amusing rattle, and my husband, who's been *longing* to meet you."

In this way did she contrive to separate Calvina from Rupert. Nor was it any surprise to find him seated next to Lysandra at one end of the table, while Calvina and Lord Ullaston were at the other.

The dinner was the final proof, if proof were needed, that Lysandra had laid herself out to impress. The first course consisted of boiled tongue, perrego turkey, haricot of mutton, fricassee of ox palates, stewed soles, roast lamb, lobster pie, and calves' heads à la turtle. The numerous side dishes included broccoli, carrots, entrée of partridges, beef olives, and turnips.

Lord Ullaston was assiduous for Calvina's comfort, ensuring that she could reach anything she fancied or sending a footman to bring her whatever was beyond her reach. He seemed determined not to meet the eye of the heavily built young man on his left, directly opposite Calvina. This was the Honorable James Ullaston, his eldest son and his heir. In between eating heartily he directed sulfurous glances down the table at his step-mother and Lord Rupert and puzzled glances at Calvina.

She partly sympathized with him. She, too, had no love for the flaunting, extravagant creature who was at this moment lightly flicking Rupert's cheek with the tip of her finger, and laughing immoderately at something he said. But there was a cold, loutish ill nature in the Honorable James's piggy eyes that almost made her pity Lysandra Ullaston.

Calvina, raised to be abstemious, still wasn't accustomed to the vast meals that society regarded as normal, and she felt she could hardly eat another thing. But when the first course was over everyone else tucked into the second with gusto. It consisted of roast woodcocks, roast larks, roast pheasants, scalloped oysters, mince pies, stewed truffles, fricassee of mushrooms, and stuffed calves' ears.

Finally the covers were removed, exposing the beautiful gleaming rosewood table, which was immediately loaded with silver epergnes filled with dried sweetmeats, elegant china baskets containing fresh, candied, and preserved fruit, and comfits and licorice in fine porcelain. To these were added small plates of olives and nuts, and glasses of shimmering jellies, creams, ices, and syllabubs. It seemed impossible that those who'd stuffed themselves on the first two courses could stuff themselves again. But the table was cleared in a remarkably short time. Calvina was rendered uncomfortable by these fine folk who gorged like pigs in swill. She observed that Rupert ate almost as little as herself, but the others wolfed down everything in sight.

When the gentlemen had joined the ladies after dinner she found herself with the Hadden twins, dressed identically, and in mischievous moods.

"There's nothing like a lady for discovering information," one of them said significantly. "If Wellington would only employ more female spies he'd thrash Bonaparte in a week."

"What do you want me to do?" Calvina asked, amused.

They joined her on the sofa, one on each side. "It's Miss Grandham," one twin explained. "Heiress. Thing is, how much of an heiress? Very important. Don't want to be taken in."

"And you're planning to marry her for her money?" Calvina said indignantly. "Shame on you!"

"What else can a poor fellow do?" asked the twin on her right pathetically. "It's all very well for *him*. He's going to be an earl. But I'm just a younger brother without a penny to my name."

"You dog! *I'm* the younger brother," said the other twin.

"Gad sir, so you are," said the first one after a moment.

"You're both impossible," Calvina said, trying to sound severe through her laughter.

"But, ma'am, you haven't thought," said the one on her right who'd turned out to be Simon, the elder. "*I've* been doing the pretty to Miss Grandham."

"Then you'll have to marry her, and serve you right," Calvina informed him heartlessly.

"No point in that," Simon explained. "He's the one who needs the heiress."

The two young men stared at each other in dismay.

"Worry about it later," George said. "Servant, ma'am." They rose together and went off in search of Miss Grandham, leaving Calvina torn between indignation and mirth.

She wasn't left alone for long. Lady Ullaston soon descended on her. "My dear Lady Rupert, I must tell you how ardently I admire your gown. So intriguingly original. I always say that those females with outrageous décolleté have quite missed the mark. The true woman is someone like yourself, with the courage to despise fashion. I'm sure that Lord Rupert supports you in this."

"I certainly dress to please my husband," Calvina said carefully, "as surely does every wife."

Lysandra gave a tinkling laugh. "Oh, when one is a

bride, enjoying one's husband's total attention, his wishes are all that count. What pleasure it is to the newly married woman to know that her husband is interested in nothing but her. I'm sure you could tell us much of these delights, ma'am."

A terrible thing happened to Calvina. Her mind went blank. She was used to the coarse nastiness of the Dalrymples, but this kind of silver-tongued spite was new to her. She was aware of Lady Ullaston watching her like a hawk, and also of the curious stares of other women who'd gathered to watch her being baited. If she didn't fight back she was lost. But nothing would come into her head and she felt she was drowning in darkness.

Then a vigorous old voice behind her said, "That's enough, Lysandra. I daresay Lady Rupert don't want to discuss her husband with outsiders."

Lady Wilmington stood there, tricked out in satins, lace, and ribbons, and her second-best wig, and looked Lysandra dead in the eyes. The younger woman fixed a smile on her face, but it didn't quite mask her fury at being called an outsider in Rupert's marriage. "In that case," she said with frosty sweetness, "I'll attend to my other guests."

She swept away, followed by her cronies, and their titters floated back to Calvina. Lady Wilmington plumped herself down on the sofa.

"So now you know," she said. "She's mad with jealousy because you carried him off before she was ready to move. Not that he'd have married her. Rupert will never lay down good money to secure a woman who's been his for the snap of his fingers. Also, he's tired of her, but she's too stupid to know that."

"I don't think he is tiring." Calvina watched as Lysandra seized possession of Rupert, laughed up into his face, and received his answering smile.

"Much you'd know!" Lady Wilmington said rudely. "Well, don't just sit there looking helpless, young woman. What are you going to do about it?"

"But what can I—I mean, Rupert and I agreed—"

"Very convenient for him," Lady Wilmington scoffed. "That doesn't mean you have to let her insult you. For heaven's sake, have you *no* woman's guile?"

"I'm afraid I haven't," Calvina said, hanging her head.

"I can see I shall have to take you in hand. Visit me tomorrow morning. Don't fail now." She bustled away.

Calvina had half hoped that Rupert would stay for at least a week, but the next day he informed her that he was again on the verge of departure. "But not until this afternoon. In the meantime, why don't you tool me around the park in the phaeton?" he asked with a smile. "I hear you've made great strides."

The thought of showing off her skill to him was so agreeable that for a moment she nearly said yes. But then the vision of him laughing down at Lysandra intervened. Calvina had left the party early, with the headache, but her husband had stayed on, playing cards.

"Thank you, my lord," she said brightly. "But I'm afraid I have an appointment this morning."

He shrugged. "Break it."

"How rude of me that would be!" She smiled. "I do not ask you to break your appointments."

"What the deuce has that got to do with it?"

"Only that it was you who said we shouldn't interfere with each other's lives."

"Very well, madam," he said curtly after a moment. "I'll depart now, since I'm clearly wasting my time and yours. Accept my good wishes for your enjoyment."

"But when will you be returning?" she faltered, half sorry now that she'd taken such a firm stand.

He shrugged. "Have you forgotten already that we live separate lives?" He saluted her ironically, and within ten minutes he'd left the house.

Defiantly Calvina had herself driven to Lady Wilmington's, where she found her hostess only half expecting her. "Didn't like it, did he?" she asked with a grim chuckle. "I thought so. I was afraid you'd yield. I'm glad you didn't. Decided not to be such a conformable wife, eh?"

"My husband once said I could enjoy myself as I pleased. I'm taking him at his word."

"My compliments. But do you know *how* to enjoy yourself?"

"I used to enjoy playing piquet with Papa," Calvina said wistfully. Catching Lady Wilmington's outraged eye upon her, she gave up the attempt. "No," she admitted, deflated.

"Then it's time you learned. Good God, whatever are you wearing?"

Together they regarded her dress of China crepe. It was high in the neck, fawn colored, with tan-satin trimmings, and in every way suitable for a morning visit on a day when there was a slight nip in the air. In fact, it was *worthy*, Calvina thought with a flash of illumination, and suddenly worthy seemed the last thing in the world that she wanted to be.

"Who's your dresser?" Lady Wilmington demanded.

Calvina explained about Sukey, who'd come with her from Bath.

"Dismiss her," Lady Wilmington said instantly. "She's no maid for a woman of fashion. You need someone well trained, like my Prudence. She despairs of me because her specialty is hairdressing, and I wear a wig."

Before Calvina could catch her breath the bell had been rung and Prudence summoned. Her eyes gleamed when she saw her mistress's guest and understood that she was going to have such exquisite raw material on which to exercise her arts. It was agreed between Prudence and Lady Wilmington that Calvina's long hair must be cut and dressed at once. She submitted reluctantly to this, but then there were arguments as to the most suitable arrangement. Prudence used the curling tongs to provide one style, then another, until they were all satisfied.

At first Calvina was slightly shocked to behold her

waist-length hair on the floor, but as she felt the sudden lightness of her head and saw how well the little feather curls became her, she took a long breath of delight.

Lady Wilmington had sent messages to the best warehouses, and soon coaches began to arrive, piled high with bolts of material. What followed was similar to when she'd chosen material at Glennister Court, except that Lady Wilmington was far haughtier than Aunt Josie, and so, for that matter, was Prudence. They both bullied the couriers without mercy and sent them running hither and thither to bring back samples of lace and satin trimmings, buttons, rosettes, spangles.

There were pattern books to be looked through, and copies of the *Ladies' Gazette*, with its numerous fashion plates. Calvina stood for what felt like hours while Prudence and Lady Wilmington discussed her as though she wasn't there. At last the orders were given, fitting sessions arranged, and she was free to enjoy a reviving cup of tea before going home, her head in a whirl.

It was settled that Prudence was to come to Glennister House by the end of the week. In the meantime there was Sukey to be considered. Calvina had no intention of dismissing her, but Prudence had declared firmly that no country bumpkin had any business in milady's boudoir.

In the end Sukey solved the problem. A tentative inquiry about how she would like to return to Glennister Court brought a whoop of delight and the plea, "Oh, yes, ma'am, if you please."

"You don't like London?" Calvina asked.

"It's well enough in its way," Sukey conceded large mindedly. "But 'ow do I know what Jeb Larkins is up to while I'm gone?"

"Who is Jeb Larkins?"

"My intended. Leastways, 'e don't zackly know as 'ow 'e's my intended, but 'e is. I intends it anyway. S'all very well 'im saying as 'ow 'e 'ent never loved another lass, but 'ow do I know if 'e be tellin' true? The world be full of designin' females, that's what. Take that Mattie Henworthy. Loosen 'er stay laces for anythin' in breeches, she would."

"But if Jeb loves you, won't he be faithful?" Calvina asked, admirably preserving her gravity.

"Faithful is as faithful does," Sukey declared darkly. "Men is men, that's what I say. If it's offered, they'll take it."

Calvina agreed that the sooner Sukey returned to reclaim her property the better. She made her a handsome gift of money to serve as a dowry and yielded to Sukey's pleas for a final visit to the Pantheon Bazaar in order to trick herself out with cheap finery.

Ladies of quality were seldom seen at the Bazaar, where glittering paste buckles could be bought for a penny, also "silver" buttons that would shine for a day until their coating wore off. There was nothing here that wouldn't have disgraced Lady Rupert's wardrobe, but Sukey was entranced, flitting from counter to counter, exclaiming, "Mattie Henworthy ain't got nothin' like *that*!" and loading up her arms with goodies.

"I think it's time we were going," Calvina said after a couple of hours.

"Yes, ma'am." Sukey was flushed with delight. "Oh my, if ever I saw such—" Her smile faded.

"Sukey, what is it?"

"My reticule, with all my money," Sukey screamed. "It's gone. Someone's stole it. It's 'im! That nasty ole varmint took it just now."

She pointed a finger at an elderly man with a long, pale face, who was just backing into the crowd, Sukey's reticule in his hand. Her shriek startled him so much that he promptly dropped the reticule before beginning to run. The crowd chased him, while Sukey pounced on her property.

"It's all there," Calvina observed as they went through the contents.

"Nasty, thievin' ole man. 'Ope they catch 'im! Don't you, ma'am?"

"Well, no," Calvina said slowly. "He looked half starved to me. You've got your money back, and I can't help hoping he escapes."

Immediately a shout went up from the crowd, followed by cries of triumph. "They got 'im!" Sukey declared.

The crowd seemed to be staring at something on the ground. Calvina pushed her way through and saw the old man lying there, breathing painfully. At once she dropped to her knees beside him and felt his cold hands. He opened his eyes and a frightened look came into them.

"Didn't mean no harm, ma'am," he said hoarsely. "Don't let 'em take me to prison again."

"No, I won't," she promised. "Lie still while I send for my carriage. Do you have a home where I can take you?"

"Trident House," he murmured, and fainted.

The constable pushed his way through the crowd, accompanied by yells of "Haul him off!"

"Now then, you—" the constable began.

"He can't hear you. The poor man is ill," Calvina said, rising to her feet and facing the policeman. "I'm going to take him home."

"He's a thief and he belongs in gaol—"

"Nonsense, of course he isn't a thief," Calvina said calmly. "My maid dropped her reticule and he very kindly picked it up for her. I'm afraid she misunderstood the situation and screamed, which made the poor man drop it again and run away. As you see, she has it now, so no theft has been committed." She kept a firm grip on Sukey's arm, lest she dispute this version. But Sukey was regarding her mistress with awe.

The constable made one last effort. "These people say he stole it," he asserted stubbornly.

"Indeed!" Calvina put all the toploftiness of which she was capable into her voice. "I am Lady Rupert Glennister. Are you going to take their word against mine?"

The constable gulped, noticing her appearance of

104

quality, and a certain indefinable something in her air. "Well, ma'am . . . if you say so. I'd better be off then."

"Find our carriage," Calvina told Sukey in a low voice. "Tell the coachman to bring it to the side entrance."

"Lor', ma'am, I can't leave you with 'im," Sukey protested.

"Do as I bid you," Calvina told her quietly but with an authority she'd never shown before. She felt suddenly confident. Years of working among the poor had left her at ease in this situation.

"Will anyone help me to lift him?" she asked the crowd.

"Best throw him into the street," a man shouted. "He's a villain."

"Don't talk nonsense," Calvina said crisply. Here, too, her air of authority made itself felt, and the man who'd shouted meekly carried the old man outside, waited until the carriage appeared, and helped to get him aboard.

Jack, the coachman, gasped when she gave their destination. "Trident House, ma'am? But that's near the docks. No place for your ladyship."

"It is where this man lives, and I have promised to convey him home."

"If he lives there it's no credit to him," Jack protested. "All the riffraff—"

"You have your orders," Calvina said, in a voice whose very gentleness contained a warning. A few minutes later they were on their way.

"Oh, ma'am, suppose 'e murders us!" Sukey wailed.

"Nonsense!" Calvina said. "He's half dead himself."

" 'E belongs in prison," Sukey said stubbornly.

"He wouldn't survive it. Prisons are terrible places, Sukey. You don't know what you're saying."

"You don't mean you've ever been in prison, ma'am?"

"Of course. Many times." Seeing the maid's eyes popping, she added, with some amusement, "Visiting, you silly girl. My father was a clergyman. I've seen worse places than you'll ever know."

She began to understand Jack's fears as they neared the docks, and their surroundings grew darker, smellier, and acquired a sinister air.

Trident House looked like a warehouse that had seen better days. A stone replica of Neptune, waving his trident, stood over the entrance and had presumably given the place its name.

No sooner had they come to a halt than the front door opened and a plainly dressed young man emerged. Calvina explained their errand and he gave a whoop of delight.

"Barnaby!" he exclaimed, peering into the carriage. "You old rogue! Miss Davison, do come. Barnaby's back."

A woman in her early thirties with a calm manner and a pleasant face came out to assist Barnaby indoors. Calvina followed them, having lost patience with Sukey, who huddled in the corner of the carriage, wailing that this was a place of doom where dreadful things happened.

Once inside she had no difficulty in recognizing a soup kitchen, such as she herself had run at one time. But it was much more besides.

"Some ladies and I have grouped together to do what we can to alleviate the terrible poverty in this city," Miss Serena Davison explained when Barnaby had been borne away to be tended. "We can provide them with nourishing food at least, and a bed for the night. The ones who are too ill to go out we keep here in our own little hospital."

A tour of the building revealed two wards, one for men and one at the top for women. They were spotlessly clean but provided little beyond basic warmth and comfort.

"We have a couple of doctors who each do a morning a week, at their own expense," Serena said. "But we are constantly short of supplies."

Calvina had instantly taken to Miss Davison. Her manners were quiet and ladylike, her dress modest but good.

Calvina had no difficulty in placing her in the ranks of parsons' kin, and Miss Davison confirmed it. Her father had been a minor cleric at Westminster Abbey. He had died, leaving his only child a competence, most of which she devoted to charitable works.

"I must thank you for returning Barnaby to us. Did he steal anything from you? If so, I'll make it good."

"Fortunately he's a most inefficient thief," Calvina said with a slight smile. "He stole my maid's reticule but dropped it almost at once. So she has lost nothing, and I was able to persuade the constable that it was all a misunderstanding."

"How kind of you!" Miss Davison said warmly. "I'm afraid Barnaby's incorrigible. He's often here, but he has an independent spirit, and after a while he roams off. I don't know what he does while he's away. He probably steals a few things and drinks too much, and when he's starving he finds his way back here. We gave him a warm coat, a gift to Trident House from a gentleman who'd hardly worn it. He was wearing it the day he left, but he's without it now, so I suppose he pawned it to buy gin."

"He didn't seem to have been drinking to me," Calvina said.

"No, which means he must have no money left at all, poor fellow. Anyway, we'll feed him until he's well. Then I suppose he'll wander off again, until he's hungry, and he'll be back."

"I think this is a wonderful place," Calvina said impulsively. "When I was working in my father's parish, I used to dream of running a place like this."

"Strictly speaking, we shouldn't be here," Serena admitted. "At one time Trident House was a warehouse for goods awaiting cargo ships coming up the river. It fell into disrepair, and the owner moved to better premises rather than make it right. We simply slipped in one night."

"How fortunate for you that it wasn't locked!"

"Oh, it was," Serena said blithely. "Luckily I was

taught to pick locks by the best cracksman in the business. At least, he said he was the best, but since he's currently in gaol, I take leave to doubt it. Anyway, the locks here presented no problem. The owner's agent grumbled, but he's made no serious attempt to evict us."

She hesitated before adding, "I had been meaning to visit you, Lady Rupert. When I heard whose daughter you were, I ventured to hope that you might assist us."

Despite her words there was a doubtful inflection in her voice. Calvina guessed that she was unsure whether to give more weight to her reputable background or her disreputable marriage. She hastened to say that she would be glad to help in any way she could.

She was forced to hurry away to prepare for a rout party she'd promised to attend that evening. On the way home she swore Sukey to silence. She couldn't feel that her destination would find favor with the other servants. She wouldn't normally have placed much reliance on Sukey's discretion, but her maid left the house next morning to catch the Bath stage.

By the afternoon Prudence had moved in and taken control of milady's boudoir. Calvina was forced to spend some time with her dresser, who'd armed herself with swatches of the materials her new mistress had chosen and together they scoured the hat shops, comparing colors.

"This hat would look well with the bombazine walking dress," Prudence pronounced in a way that brooked no argument. As proof she held up the piece of dark red bombazine, and the matter was settled.

But while she paraded in new clothes under Prudence's critical eye, Calvina's thoughts were at Trident House. After a couple of days she managed to slip away unnoticed and hired a hackney to take her to the docks.

She still had much left over of Rupert's generous allowance, and was able to make a gift of money. But her temperament demanded active involvement, and she stayed to help out. This was familiar work. She knew any number of nourishing, inexpensive recipes. She was also a skilled nurse, able to clean and bind up wounds, and make herbal remedies.

She found a deep satisfaction that had been missing from her life recently. At first she'd found pleasure in her luxurious existence. After drudgery and spite at the Dalrymples', it was bliss to be pampered for a while. But her conscience would not allow her to enjoy idle ease for long.

"I wonder sometimes what I'm doing in the midst of luxury," she confided to Serena Davison. "I'm sure Papa would be shocked if he could see me now. I feel I should find a way of giving it all up."

"On no account in the world," Serena said instantly. "It's so hard to interest society ladies in our work. They dole out money sometimes, but they don't interest themselves closely, as you are doing. Perhaps your example will encourage them."

"I wish I felt more hopeful of that," Calvina observed wryly. "Sometimes I think all that is necessary to be a great lady of the ton is to be greedy, frivolous, and think about nothing but your own family's advancement."

"But you were called to your present position to serve some purpose," Serena said gravely. "Your husband must have loved you very much to marry you so impulsively. Through that love you will affect his life, just as he has affected yours."

"Of course," Calvina said awkwardly. It was impossible to explain to this earnest woman that Rupert didn't love her at all, and that these days he seemed to have forgotten her.

The servants had begun by regarding Calvina askance, but she'd won the liking of most of them. The most notable exception was Mrs. Andrews, the housekeeper. She had been with the Glennister family all her life, and thought that a young woman with neither rank nor money of her own was wholly unworthy of Lord Rupert.

Without ever crossing the line to outright insolence she allowed her views to appear in her manner. Calvina had tried to make a friend of her, but all her efforts had failed against the rock of Mrs. Andrews's resentment.

When she discovered her mistress's habit of slipping away at odd hours, sometimes at night, with neither a footman nor maid in attendance, she was bitter in her disapproval. Had her manner been more courteous Calvina might have confided in her, but Mrs. Andrews made the mistake of lecturing her about her "unseemly conduct." Calvina's temper flared up and the end was that the housekeeper flounced off indignantly, more than ever convinced that Lord Rupert's bride was unfit for her position.

It became a malicious game with her to spy on Calvina in a vain attempt to discover her secret. Calvina, with equal determination, refused to give her the satisfaction, and always contrived to slip away.

But there was still room in her life for pleasure. Balls, parties, and Venetian breakfasts became even more delightful now that she could enjoy them with a clear conscience. And under Prudence's care she presented a new and dazzling beauty to the world.

It was Prudence's idea to dress her mistress's short hair *à la Médusee*, a style that had a touch of insouciance, half-cheeky, half-seductive. She planned to show it for the first time at Almack's. While Prudence worked skillfully, Calvina sat meekly in her ball dress, wishing that Rupert would return and see her new appearance.

Suddenly she heard a small commotion from below, the sound of someone being admitted through the front door and talking in the hall. She told Prudence to finish her hair quickly, and hurried out to greet Rupert.

But it wasn't Rupert who stood there. Calvina checked herself, suppressing a stab of disappointment before going down to her visitor. Then he looked up and her delight was partially restored.

"Ninian!" she cried, flying the rest of the way down.

"Oh, my dear friend, it's so good to see you again." She gave him an eager hug, which he returned willingly. "But what brings you here?" she asked. "Rupert told me you never came to London because you couldn't bear to leave Glennister Court."

"I have some papers for him to sign, and I wanted to see how you were both managing."

"I'm in high gig," she assured him.

"That is evident." Ninian was taking in her gown of deep blue-silk taffeta, figured with silver and trimmed with floss silk. "I hardly know you, you're so fine."

"You don't think I've gone too far, do you?" she asked anxiously.

"You look like a lady of fashion, which is right. What does Rupert think of the transformation?"

"He hasn't seen it yet. He's been out of town these three weeks."

"You mean he's not here now?" Ninian asked, frowning. "That's a shame. I'd counted on seeing him. But you could send him a message?"

A little color crept into Calvina's cheeks as she said awkwardly, "I don't know—that is, I'm not certain—we don't hang on each other's sleeves."

"Yes, but surely—" Ninian checked himself. He was watching her carefully. "I'm glad I came," he said gently.

It flashed across her mind that his real reason for this trip was concern for her welfare. That was absurd, of course, for Rupert was treating her well, very well. In fact, she had nothing at all to complain of. She tried to reassure her companion with her brightest smile, but it didn't banish the troubled look in his eyes.

Over dinner he made her talk about herself. He seemed interested in the smallest details, and the conviction grew in Calvina that something was worrying him. But her questions met with hurried disclaimers, followed by a determined turning of the conversation.

"You're not eating," he said at one point.

"I seldom eat much before I dance," Calvina explained

quickly. The truth was disappointment had made her appetite desert her.

When the clock struck nine she remembered that the twins would soon be calling to take her to Almack's. "But I need not go. I'd rather stay here and talk to you."

"Why should you give up your enjoyments?" Ninian demanded. "If Rupert can—" He checked himself hastily. "I mean, he left you a free agent."

"Come with us," Calvina urged, pretending not to notice this slip. "I'm sure you get very little pleasure."

He hesitated, but after a while allowed himself to be persuaded. When the twins arrived they found Calvina with a young gentleman of grave demeanor, soberly if correctly dressed in knee breeches. Concealing their dismay, they welcomed Ninian into their carriage, and the four of them went on their way to Almack's.

It wasn't lost on Ninian that Calvina was the center of attention as soon as she arrived. Young blades converged on her, to the chagrin of many damsels, and soon every dance was taken. No one was as gay as Calvina that evening, no one danced so lightly or so hectically, no one else's laughter was so determinedly bright.

After a while she began to feel the effects of eating so little at supper. The room was hot and she was constantly on her feet. In the refreshment room she drank some tea and ate some small cakes, but then the giddy whirl began again.

The next waltz was with Ninian, who took one look at her flushed face and glittering eyes, and proposed that they sit down. "For I'm sure you are tired."

"Tired? Not at all," Calvina responded, laughing merrily. "I'm enjoying myself hugely. I spent so many years living quietly that this is a delightful change for me. Don't you feel the same?"

"I find that I can't take any pleasure in tonight," he replied gravely.

If only she could admit that she felt the same, that her head was aching, and so was her heart. But she was trapped on a treadmill of gaiety, and there was nothing to do but dance to the finish. If only the room weren't so hot, and everything whirling about her. She began to sway, feeling Ninian's arms holding her up. The next moment his grip tightened, his face was above hers, calling her name in alarm as she slumped against him.

Dizzily she was aware of his assisting her from the room into a small antechamber. Lady Wilmington appeared with smelling salts. Calvina gagged on the pungent odor and struggled to sit up.

"I promise you I am well," she gasped.

"Of course you are," Lady Wilmington said robustly. "Most natural thing in the world."

It dawned on Calvina that the old woman thought she was with child. Everyone else thought so, too, if the smiles she saw as she left the ballroom were any guide. She was too sick and weary to correct the false impression, and besides, what could she say? That after four months of marriage she was still a virgin?

Ninian took his leave next day. "I've left the papers on Rupert's desk," he said.

"Must you really go?" Calvina begged. "It was so nice to have you here."

"You need to rest now."

"But, Ninian, I'm not—what everybody thinks," she said.

"No? Forgive me, but you can hardly be sure."

It was impossible to tell him just how sure she could be. "Last night I danced too much and ate too little. Gay to dissipation, in fact. That was all."

"Whatever the reason, you must look after yourself. I'll leave you to recover your strength, but I'll come back. Often. And, Calvina"—he seemed suddenly overcome with awkwardness—"take care."

"I always do," she protested with a smile.

"No, I mean more than that. I mean—I mean be careful. And if you're ever in any trouble or danger, send for me and I'll be with you as fast as I can."

"Danger?" she echoed. "What danger could I possibly be in?"

He gave a forced smile. "Nothing, of course. I'm just being overcautious."

"If you see Rupert, be sure to tell him what a good time I was having last night," she commanded him with a merry smile.

She won no answering smile. Ninian regarded her with an odd look in his eyes, before saying quietly, "I don't think I could make myself tell him that." He saluted her with a kiss on the cheek and departed.

Chapter Seven

Over the next few days Calvina discovered that all London seemed to know that she was "in an interesting condition." She denied it, saying truthfully that she'd been overcome by the heat, but as she couldn't give the real reason, she had to settle for being generally disbelieved. People smiled kindly, showing that they understood that she might not be ready to make an announcement. Doubtless Ninian had thought the same.

Lysandra Ullaston paid a morning call and uttered civilities for a quarter of an hour while her eyes raked her hostess's slim figure up and down. Nor was it lost on her that the sedate young woman she'd despised so carelessly was now tricked out in the highest kick of fashion. Calvina's gown of white-jaconet embroidered with tiny leaves could only have come from a modiste of the first stare, and her glowing curls had clearly been turned out by an experienced dresser.

Calvina played her part in the conversation. Her inspiration was beginning to flag when she remembered that Lord Ullaston was not in the best of health. She commiserated with her guest on this fact, and Lysandra broke into an impassioned speech about her devotion to her lord. Calvina didn't believe a word of it, but she was astounded by the look in Lysandra's eyes. It was one of sheer terror.

Calvina was fast discovering that she had a frivolous side. She still found her real satisfaction in working at

Trident House, and the friends she made there were eac[h]
worth a hundred of the wealthy nonentities she met i[n]
society. Nor did she merely include Miss Davison and
her assistants. Some of those on the receiving end of
charity delighted her. Barnaby was her especial favorite.
Now his strength was returning he would greet her with a
cheeky gleam in his eye and engage her in chitchat until
she was obliged to shoo him away in order to get any
work done.

Sometimes there were night expeditions to find the
poor where they lay in the streets, collapsed with hunger
or huddled in doorways. Calvina would go out with the
others, refusing to be chickenhearted about the terrible
things she would see. But Barnaby, who'd once been a
gentleman's gentleman, had all the notion of her consequence that she lacked, and would accompany her as her
champion and protector.

But with all this, she still nurtured a childish desire to
go to a Covent Garden masquerade. These were colorful,
vulgar occasions, and to attend them wasn't good ton.
But since everyone wore masks she felt she could take
the risk. The twins gallantly agreed to squire her. Their
activities sometimes lay apart these days, since George
was not only deep in a courtship of Miss Grandham, but
actually showed signs of forming a genuine passion for
her. Simon sensibly avoided the lady entirely, for fear
that he should lose his heart in the same place as his
brother's, as in the past.

"Devilish awkward that would be," he confided to
Calvina.

"It's time you were following his example," she
told him.

"Whatever for?" he asked in some alarm.

"You're going to be the earl. You have responsibilities."

"No such thing. If George marries and sets up his
nursery, his son can be my heir. No need for both of us to
get legshackled." He'd grown pale at the prospect and
hastily restored himself with a large brandy.

Just now Miss Grandham had gone to visit relatives in the country, where a viscount was also invited. This cast George into gloom, as it was clear that the Grandham family meant to engage her to the viscount, if possible. He gladly consented to attend the masquerade, to distract his mind from dark thoughts of plots and conspiracies. On the night of the masquerade, the three of them set off together, attired in masks and dominoes, the capacious cloaks that could conceal or reveal as much as the wearer chose.

The seats of the opera house had been removed, and the floor boarded over, turning it into a kind of ballroom. Around the side were ranged the boxes, where private little groups could enjoy a supper of champagne and delicacies. Calvina was enjoying herself hugely, but she didn't let herself forget the time. She'd promised to go to Trident House to spend some hours on duty in the little infirmary. An outbreak of influenza had decimated the helpers, so it was vital that she keep her word. Like Cinderella, she must vanish at midnight. She'd left a change of raiment in the little cloakroom. After putting on her plain dress, it would be easy to slip away and hire a hackney from the rank.

It wasn't long before Calvina's party was joined by several of her other admirers who took over the boxes on either side, ruthlessly ejecting anyone who'd gotten there first. She was completely surrounded by a circle of young men eager to offer her champagne or supper, to dance with her, or merely to prostrate themselves at her feet.

One who actually did so was the Honorable Elwyn Renton, an aspiring poet. An astonishingly handsome boy with dreamy eyes and an otherworldly air, he'd long since taken Calvina as his muse and would stretch out on the floor, declaring that only in this position could he write his best verse. The others were scornful, but since Calvina permitted these unorthodox attentions they had to put up with stepping over him.

"I say, who's that game little pullet?" the Honorable Henry Leverton demanded, lifting his opera glasses for a closer view. "She seems to have nearly every man in the place hanging on her sleeve."

"Be careful, Lev," warned the man lounging carelessly in his box, drinking brandy. "Those masks are a take-in. Remember last time, and what a devil of a job I had to rescue you."

"Damn you, Rupert, why must you always be a cynic?"

"Life, dear boy! Life."

"I tell you, that one's as much a beauty without her mask as with it. You can see by her mouth."

His companion sat forward and took the glasses. "Leave it to a connoisseur," he commanded. "I'll tell you if she's up to standard." The next moment he grew very still, his eyes fixed on the woman in the far box, laughing and flirting.

"Well, what do you think?" Leverton asked impatiently.

"What I think, my boy, is that you'd better go nowhere near her."

"But I tell you—"

"And I tell *you* to keep your distance."

Lord Rupert hadn't raised his voice, but something in it made a chill run up the younger man's spine. He felt, as he later told his awed cronies, that another word would see him turned into a toad.

"If you say so," he said sulkily.

Lord Rupert rose and slipped on his mask. Through the slits Leverton noted that his eyes had lost their terrible look, which emboldened him to say, "I see what it is. You want her for yourself."

"Precisely." Lord Rupert's smile was like the flashing of a blade. "And I permit no rivals. Spread the word."

Leverton continued to watch through his glasses and saw the moment when Rupert entered the far box. A silence seemed to fall, and the young blade who'd been kissing Calvina's hand stopped hastily. Then a redheaded little lovebird with a purple-spangled mask winked at Leverton, and he forgot everything else.

Gradually Calvina's box emptied, save only for the poet who remained oblivious to all but his own inspiration.

"*Goddess of the stars,*" he intoned. "Or *Goddess of the night.* What do you think?"

"I think you'll depart now, if you know what's good for you," Rupert declared.

"What's good for me is to lie here at my angel's feet— I say, that's it! *Angel of the stars—* or *night.*"

Calvina's heart began to beat faster as she easily recognized her husband despite his mask, but she allowed no agitation to appear. Her eyes, behind the slits in her frosted mask, were gleaming. "I think 'angel of the night' is delightful," she told the poet provocatively.

"I think it's nauseating," her ungallant companion observed. "Be gone, sir."

The Honorable Elwyn looked longingly at his angel— or goddess, he hadn't quite decided. "Do *you* wish me to depart?" he asked in a beseeching tone. "Ah, say not that I must be torn from my bright star."

"But I haven't said it." Calvina chuckled, with a provocative eye on her husband. "Stay and write couplets to me."

Either Elwyn hadn't recognized Rupert, or he was brave to the point of foolhardiness, for he propped himself on one elbow, shook out his raven locks, and clasped a hand over his heart.

"Lay your beloved fingers on my brow," he begged. "Your touch shall cause my muse to soar, and I shall drown in inspiration, drown in beauty, drown in love— *Hey!*"

"Drown in champagne." Rupert set down the bottle and hauled the sodden poet to his feet. Elwyn was gasping and spluttering through the champagne dripping down his face. His coat was wet and his appearance was more bedraggled than romantic.

119

"Philistine!" he shrieked. "You have robbed the world of a glorious poem."

"Another word and I'll rob it of the poet, too," Rupert declared, propelling the young man irresistibly out of the door, and closing it firmly behind him. Calvina was convulsed with laughter.

Lord Rupert drew up a chair and sat beside her. His eyes were coolly ironical. "You'll forgive me, ma'am, for intruding on you, but for a moment you reminded me of someone I knew."

"Is it a close likeness, sir, or only in passing?"

"In passing, I think. In fact, now I come closer, I see you're not really like her at all."

"Obviously not a lady you've seen recently?"

"Not as much as I should have done," he conceded. "I'm shamed by my own neglectfulness."

"No doubt she's been wearing the willow for you all this time?"

"I rather fancy not," he said slowly. "In fact, I'd meant to get to know her better"—his lips curved in a significant smile—"but now I think I'd prefer to know you."

Calvina cast down her eyes in a parody of demureness and fluttered her fan. "Alas, sir, my time is quite taken up. I have so many friends—"

"They will yield to me, I assure you, ma'am."

She was enjoying this verbal sparring. They were themselves, and yet not themselves, hidden behind masks that brought the freedom to say what they pleased. "And suppose *I* do not choose to yield to you?" she asked.

He leaned forward so that his breath touched her cheek. "You will. The time is coming when you must."

Tremors went through her at a certain note in his voice, and she smiled enigmatically. "Who can say what fate has in store?"

"Some men make their own fate. I have always made mine. I insist on it."

"I perceive you're not a man to be trifled with."

His eyes gleamed through the slits. "How astute of you."

"May I know your name?"

"They call me the devil," he said softly.

"Then devil take you, sir," she murmured.

"He will, in his own good time."

For a moment she wondered if Rupert hadn't recognized her, but his eyes were sharp with intelligence. He knew who she was but he'd chosen, for reasons of his own, to play this game.

The band had struck up a waltz. Everywhere couples were throwing themselves into each other's arms, in the most indecorous fashion. "Dance with me," Rupert said, holding out his hand to her in a manner that was more of a command than a request.

As soon as they were on the floor he took her in his arms, holding her close as they waltzed. Calvina felt herself grow breathless. He studied her left hand, held in his right. "You wear no wedding ring," he remarked.

"I removed it for reasons of safety," she said quickly. "In such a crush as this—"

"Ah, yes. And a wedding ring is very revealing, is it not? Does your husband know that you attend such improper events?"

"If he were here, he could know. But he's been out of town for some time."

"More fool him, to let you wander about at liberty. Does he neglect you?"

She gave a merry laugh. "I care nothing for his neglect. As long as I don't ask about *his* life, I'm free to do as I please."

"I doubt that," he remarked calmly.

"Oh yes, indeed! He said—"

"Whatever he may have said in a hasty moment, no man likes his wife to enjoy herself too much without him."

"You think he didn't really mean it?" she asked lightly. "What a shabby fellow!"

"I begin to think your husband is indeed a shabby fellow," Rupert said slowly.

He swirled her around and around before she had time to reply. She was dancing at a giddy speed, yet she had the strangest sensation of not moving at all, but keeping still, enclosed in a cocooned world with Rupert, while the rest of creation spun about them. She could see his mouth, smiling sensually beneath his mask, and his eyes through the slits had a disturbing gleam. Her pulse quickened. Every part of her being was alive with excitement.

Suddenly she felt everything grow still and quiet. His arm steadied her as he brought the dance to a halt, and she realized that the music and the other dancers had vanished. Her head was still spinning.

"Where did they all go?" she asked dreamily.

His mouth was close to hers. "I made them vanish with a wave of my hand."

Her mind had cleared enough to understand that he had simply danced her out of the ballroom into a quiet corridor, but she clung to the enchanting illusion.

"You cast a spell?" she whispered.

"The spell that holds you and me is the most powerful spell in the world. Did I not say so, once before, to—one who looked like you?"

"Long ago . . . in another life," she said hazily.

He kissed her lingeringly. "Another life, another time," he said against her mouth.

"I was another woman," she murmured, slipping her hand behind his head and kissing him back.

"Then you were merely delightful. I promised myself that you'd be mine one day. Now you're an entrancing witch, and I desire you to madness . . ."

They were no longer in the corridor, but in a small private room, dimly lit by a few candles. Calvina wasn't sure how or when he'd taken her there. She was consumed by passion, wholly given up to the delight of being in Rupert's arms, the object of his desire. His kisses ravished her.

"Come," he said imperiously. "It is time for us to go."

"Where will you take me?"

"To the moon and the stars, or wherever you wish."

She retained enough of her wits to say, "I cannot go home with a stranger, sir."

"I am no stranger to you, madam. And before this night is out I shall be even less of a stranger. Come!"

But the next instant they were startled by a tinkling sound from somewhere in the room. "What's that?" she asked hazily.

"There must be a clock in here. It's striking midnight."

"Midnight!" She retreated from him as memory came flooding back. "I must go."

"You'll go nowhere except with me." His voice made her pulses throb. She longed to go with him. At that moment passion seemed more important than anything else in the world. But she wasn't Calvin Bracewell's daughter for nothing. She'd given Serena her solemn word, and it must be kept, despite her own longings.

"I regret, sir, that I must leave you," she said in a shaking voice.

"I forbid it. You belong to me. What can matter more than that?"

"My promise. I gave my word to—" She hesitated. This was no time to speak of Trident House.

"To whom?" he asked. "Another man? That I will not allow."

"You don't understand—"

"I understand that we were made for each other, this night." He drew her close for a lingering kiss, his lips persuading her with the subtlety of the devil. "This night, and many others . . ." he murmured.

Calvina fought with temptation. Could it be wrong to put her husband first? Yes, replied her conscience firmly. She was needed elsewhere, and this was mere self-indulgence.

"Let me go," she begged.

"Never." His lips made a line of fire down her neck.

Her will was drowning in her desire. In another moment she would yield, forgetting everything but him.

But then rescue came in an unlikely form. There was a crash as the door to the little room was flung open by others bent on the same errand.

"Take yourselves off!" Rupert snapped.

"Fair's fair!" said a drunken male voice. "Room for all in this little love nest."

The room was filling up fast as at least three couples crowded in. Rupert cursed but abandoned the argument. He'd been about to leave anyway.

"Come!" He held out his hand to his wife.

But she'd vanished.

"Your little lovebird's flown the coop," one of the men said with a leering chuckle. "Never mind. Plenty more here."

"Be damned to you," Rupert said with a soft venom that made them back away from him. Turning on his heel, he left the room.

He soon realized that it was pointless to search for her. The little witch had given him the slip very thoroughly. But then, he thought, his temper cooling, this was doubtless a stratagem to inflame his desire still further. The Calvina he'd married would never have thought of it. But the Calvina who'd kissed him tonight was a new and completely unexpected woman. He had only to go home, where the "stranger" would be waiting for him. Smiling to himself, he set off.

But when he reached Berkeley Square he discovered that his wife's room was empty. A casual inquiry to Prudence produced the information that her ladyship had gone to Covent Garden and had said she would be very late getting home. Rupert refused to arouse speculation by revealing what he knew. Nor did he choose to expose himself to ridicule by questioning the other servants.

He waited, listening for the sound of the porter admitting Calvina through the front door. It never came. But at last he heard the door of his wife's room open and close softly, then the murmur of voices as Prudence undressed her mistress.

He could have gone in and questioned her, but the role of baffled husband did not appeal to him. He was left with no choice but to be patient, although his anger was growing by the minute. Calvina's words about a promise were assuming a new and ominous aspect. For the first time he wondered whether she had actually recognized him at all. He'd been in London for a day before attending the masquerade, but that was enough for the rumor of his wife's pregnancy to reach him. His trust of her was so complete that he'd shrugged and discounted it, but now an ugly look came into his eyes.

Sukey might have thrown light on the mystery, had she been present. But at that very moment Sukey was enjoying her wedding night, where her ripe charms inspired a display of skill from Jeb Larkins that first aroused her suspicions, and then made her declare blissfully that that was *summat*, and no mistake.

Calvina slept little that night. She had returned in the early hours, troubled by a talk with Miss Davison.

"The thing I dreaded most has happened," Serena had confided worriedly. "The owner of Trident House means to sell. He's offered it to us if we can match the price, but it's a thousand pounds and I see no chance of obtaining it."

"How much time do we have?" Calvina asked. "I can give you what I have left from this month's allowance, but it's only five hundred."

"Because your kind heart has made you give so much to us already," Serena said warmly. "Sadly, we only have until the end of next week. Then we must either buy or leave."

"No matter. I'll speak to my husband tomorrow, and get an advance on next month's allowance."

"Will he give you five hundred pounds, just like that?"

Calvina's lips had curved as she remembered the masquerade, only a few hours ago. "I think he will," she said.

She hurried down the next morning, longing to see Rupert, with the consciousness of last night in his eyes. How would he look at her? What would he say?

She'd doubted her own wisdom in slipping away abruptly, but a night of reflection had convinced her that he was just a little too sure of himself. A period of uncertainty would do him the world of good. She was smiling as she entered the breakfast room.

But there she was met by the butler with the news that his lordship had breakfasted early and departed. He was not expected back until that evening.

Calvina took a deep breath and tried to stifle a childish feeling of disappointment. Rupert was either offended at her desertion last night, or he suspected her of playing a cat-and-mouse game with him, and was retaliating in kind. In that case, there might still be some hope.

But when she saw him that evening she knew that he was playing no game. She entered his study to find him frowning. His brow lightened at the sight of her, but a hint of darkness remained far back in his eyes.

"I've come to beg a favor," she said, smiling.

"Name it."

"Will you give me an advance on next month's allowance?"

"Run into debt, Calvina?" he asked with a quizzical look.

"Not exactly . . ."

"Then why this sudden state of poverty?"

"I can't explain. If you could just let me have five hundred pounds, and take it out of next month . . ."

"What is it? A new dress to delight me?"

"Please, Rupert."

His smile vanished. "Can't you tell me what it's for?"

"No, I—I can't."

"Secrets from your husband?" he asked, and although

his tone was light there was something in it that warned her to be careful.

"It doesn't matter," she said hastily. "It's nothing, nothing at all."

"On the contrary. It is much that you don't feel you can trust me."

"But *you* do not trust *me*," she pointed out.

She waited for his disclaimer, but it didn't come. Instead, he asked after a moment, "Would Toby Aylesbury be in London, by any chance?"

"Of course not," she declared hotly. "How can you believe such a thing of me?"

"Are you quite sure that he isn't, and that you never think of him?"

"I'm quite sure he isn't in London," she replied.

"And do you never think of him?"

Calvina took a nervous breath. "I will not tell you my thoughts, my lord," she replied with dignity. "I believed that was understood. I'm sorry to have troubled you about this matter." Before he could answer she'd turned and left the room.

Left alone, Lord Rupert brooded in silence, an ugly look in his eyes. He was remembering how his wife had slipped away from the masquerade, leaving him to arrive home, seeking her. He was thinking, too, of the rumors that had reached him since his return to London, and which he'd discounted, because he trusted her. A feeling of cold rage was overtaking him, and if she had been there to see his face, even she might have quailed.

Calvina had hurried up to her room. She was shaking and puzzled by her own behavior. Why had she not simply told Rupert what he wanted to know? Her work among the poor would probably please him. It was suitable for the impression he wanted her to convey.

Then she understood why she'd kept her secret so stubbornly. What she did at Trident House was in earnest. She would never allow it to become part of the game Rupert was playing with society. Barnaby and the others mattered too much to be used in that way.

Meanwhile, she was left without the money, but after some serious thought, and some heartache, she discovered the answer to that problem.

She dined alone that night, Rupert having departed without explanation. Afterward she slipped out alone as usual and went to Trident House, to assure Serena that the money would be available in a couple of days.

"Then your husband has come to our rescue," Serena said jubilantly. "Did he mind your asking him?"

"My husband is a very generous man," Calvina said, not choosing to disclose more.

She helped out with supper, chatting to the people she now thought of as friends. When Serena told her that her hackney had arrived she was unprepared. "He's an hour early," she said in surprise. "I told him not to come until midnight."

"Never mind. You've done enough. Go home and rest now."

Her preferred driver was usually standing by the open door of the carriage, ready to hand her in. But tonight he sat muffled on the box, his head sunk in scarves, while a hacking cough came from him.

"You poor fellow," Calvina said sympathetically. "No wonder you want to get home quickly. Let's hurry then."

As soon as she closed the door after her the hackney took off at a fast pace. She clung to the sides, thinking that the driver must be sadly ill to drive like this. Then the hackney swung, took a corner much too fast, and she was thrown violently to the floor. She scrambled up, gasping, but was immediately thrown again, this time striking her head.

She fought for something to cling to, but now they were traveling at a terrifying speed, and she was tossed this way and that like a rag doll. For a moment she wondered if the driver had collapsed and fallen right off the box, but she could clearly hear the sound of the whip being cracked to urge on the horses. Someone was doing this to her on purpose.

She managed to struggle up, clinging first to the seat and then to the straps. Holding on for dear life she pushed down the window and looked out into the darkness. She could see the horses galloping hell-for-leather, their manes streaming out behind them.

"Stop!" she screamed. *"Stop!"*

But another crack of the whip was her only answer, and it seemed to her frantic imagination that the horses raced faster still. A wild lurch sent her flying to the far side of the carriage to land, sprawling, on the floor. She tried to keep a clear head but fear and horror were rising in her breast, threatening to overwhelm her. Who could hate her enough to be so malevolent?

Then she set her chin. Whoever was trying to harm her would fail. If the driver wouldn't stop, then she would jump. She concentrated as they went around a bend. The driver took it at reckless speed, but even he had to slow down a little. Calvina hauled herself to her feet and managed to look out the window again. Another bend was approaching. Taking a deep breath, she unlatched the carriage door, and stood holding it loose, clinging on for dear life. As she felt the violent swerve she let go of the handle so that the door swung open and she was hurled through the gap.

She landed on all fours on the pavement. The crash as she hit the flagstones shook her badly, but she retained enough presence of mind to look at the carriage, hurtling on without her, until it disappeared.

There was no time to think of anything but getting home safely. To her vast relief she was in an area that she knew, having driven through it many times in her own carriage. She got painfully to her feet and began to trudge in the right direction. In this select area she stood a good chance of getting to safety without being accosted. She could only pray that she might slip home undetected.

It was half a mile to Berkeley Square, and every step made her shaken body ache. At last the house came into view, and she limped the last few yards, praying that the side door would still be open as she'd left it. To her relief, it was, and she slipped quietly inside and up the back stairs.

It was a relief to get into bed and stretch out her battered limbs. She tried to think but couldn't. More than physical pain was the bewilderment of wondering who wanted to hurt her and why.

She wondered how late Rupert would be, and suddenly found herself longing for him. She remembered how comforting his arms could be, and wanted them now, holding her tightly against his broad chest. He'd held her like that when she'd had hysterics, and they had passed away in the warmth of his embrace. If only he were here to hold her now, and make her fears disappear.

She sat up in bed, alerted by a sound from the corridor outside. There were footsteps passing her door, heading toward Rupert's bedroom. She hustled on her satin peignoir, ran to the door, and pulled it open. She was about to call Rupert's name eagerly, but the word died on her lips.

The corridor was dark, lit only by a few wall candles. In the deep shadows she could make out little of her husband beyond the glitter of his eyes and a strange expression on his face. She could almost have thought he was surprised to see her. But more than that was a look of definite hostility.

"Good evening, madam," he said distantly.

"Rupert, I—"

"I trust that your party of pleasure was agreeable? I do not recall your telling me where you were going."

"I—"

His voice was silky. "Or perhaps you stayed at home?"

"I did go out, but—only for a little while. I returned sooner than I expected. There were reasons—"

130

"I'm quite sure there were. I do not inquire into them. Good night, madam."

"Good night," she said bleakly, withdrawing into her room and shutting the door.

Chapter Eight

Returning home unexpectedly late one afternoon Rupert discovered that his wife had gone out. He shrugged and returned to his study, where he was accosted by Mrs. Andrews, puffed up and full of virtuous self-importance. "I'm sorry to trouble you, sir, but I felt it was my duty."

"Can't you wait and tell her ladyship? Where is she, by the way?"

"I don't know, sir. No more does anyone else in the house."

"What instructions did she give in the stables?"

"None, sir. Her ladyship doesn't take her carriage when she goes out on these visits."

Lord Rupert was silent for a long moment, apparently examining his nails. When he spoke again his voice held a warning. "And was this what you felt it your duty to tell me?"

"No, sir. It's her ladyship's pearl brooch, the one she sets such store by. It must have been stolen."

"What do you mean, 'must have been'? It's no part of your duties to concern yourself with my wife's jewelry."

"No, sir, but I've just seen that selfsame brooch in the window of a pawnshop, and how it got there, if it weren't stolen—"

"That's enough!" Lord Rupert's soft voice held a note that was enough to silence the housekeeper. "Who else knows about this?"

"Prudence. She thought the brooch was being cleaned. That was what her ladyship told her."

"What is the direction of this pawnshop?" Mrs. Andrews gave it. "Very well, you may return to your duties."

Lord Rupert remained very still when she'd left, his face expressionless. At last he summoned his carriage and gave the coachman the direction of the pawnshop.

The pawnbroker was an ill-favored little man, whose small eyes gleamed at the sight of a wealthy client. He produced the pearl brooch, which Rupert had no difficulty recognizing as the one he'd retrieved from the Dalrymples. A feeling of nausea rose in him at the thoughts that possessed his brain. He tried to shut them off. Knowing Calvina's character, he'd persuaded himself that the rumors of her pregnancy must be mistaken. It was impossible that she was playing him false in the extreme meaning of the term. But her sentimental attachment to that milksop, as he thought of Toby, was another matter. It was intangible, yet it wouldn't be broken, and it drove him to madness.

Rupert was in touch with Aunt Josie, and the steward who cared for his lodgings in Bath, and he knew a great deal about how the modest Aylesbury fortune was slipping away. He knew also that, despite Calvina's denial, Toby was in London, though whether she'd misled him by accident or design he wasn't certain.

He paid twice what the brooch was worth and left the shop tight-lipped.

He saw coachman Jack looking at him expectantly and gave a wry shrug. He'd known Jack all his life and trusted him totally. "I suppose you have no light to throw on the mystery?" he asked.

"What mystery, guv'nor?" A raised eyebrow was Rupert's only response. "You mean her la'ship? Not unless she's gone back to that place."

"What place?"

"Place I took her with the cove she found in the Pantheon Bazaar. Insisted on taking him home."

"To Glennister House?"

"No, guv'nor. His home."

"Take me there," Lord Rupert said quickly, and got in.

It took half an hour to reach Trident House, and as the streets grew darker and more sinister he was half inclined to think Jack had mistaken the way, which Jack hotly denied.

"It was Trident House and no mistake," he insisted. "We'll be there in half a mo'."

The name Trident House suggested a grandeur that was wholly belied by their increasingly mean surroundings. Rupert's bewilderment increased when they pulled up outside the warehouse.

"Here?" he demanded.

"True as my life, guv'nor."

The front door opened and a quietly dressed young woman came out onto the step. "I am Miss Davison. May I help you?"

"I'm seeking Lady Rupert Glennister," he informed her, half expecting to hear that they'd never heard of his wife. But Miss Davison smiled.

"Please come in. She is occupied at the moment, but I'll send her a message."

The nature of Trident House was revealed to him as soon as he stepped inside. In a room to one side of the corridor he could see food being ladled out of vats.

"Some of the people here actually have work, but no place to live," Miss Davison told him. "They sleep here and contribute part of their earnings for our upkeep. Thanks to your generosity the fear of eviction has been lifted from us."

"Thanks to me?"

"Was it not you? Lady Rupert said she was sure you would help us find the necessary sum, and when she brought the money—oh, dear! I fear I should not have spoken."

"On the contrary, I think you should tell me everything."

Miss Davison related the tale simply, starting with the

134

day Calvina had brought Barnaby home, and finishing with the money she'd provided to help buy the building. It became clear to Rupert how his wife had been spending her time during her mysterious absences from home. Satisfaction warred with chagrin that she had chosen to exclude him.

"This is Barnaby," Serena said, glancing up at a lanky, elderly man in the doorway. "He will take you to Lady Rupert."

"Don't know as how I will." Barnaby sniffed. "She's busy."

"Nonetheless I should be grateful if you would conduct me to her," Rupert said.

The old reprobate looked him up and down. He had no great opinion of lords. "I can't take everyone up there," he said suspiciously. "How do I know she wants to see you?"

Rupert's lips twitched. "I am her husband."

"So you say!"

Serena covered her eyes with her hand. "Barnaby has appointed himself Lady Rupert's champion," she said in a faint voice.

"So I see," Rupert said gravely, although his eyes danced. "But I assure you, sir, I am the lady's husband."

" 'Spose you are, that don't mean she wants to see you," Barnaby replied with invincible logic.

"Unfortunately that seems to be true," Rupert murmured.

"I'll conduct you upstairs myself," Serena declared.

"No need to trouble yourself, ma'am." Rupert scribbled something hastily and handed it to her. "Barnaby's escort will suit me admirably. My wife's champion must always be a friend of mine."

Barnaby seemed a little confused by this idea, and while he was still trying to work it out, found himself somehow leading the way upstairs. Rupert followed, managing to be out of earshot before Serena could recover from the sight of the banker's draft he'd given her and voice her thanks.

He saw Calvina as soon as he reached the top floor, but she didn't see him. She was sitting by the bed of an elderly man, supporting him in her arms while he drank laboriously from a cup she held to his lips. The man said something, and as she responded her face was illuminated by such a smile that Rupert drew in his breath. She was totally absorbed in what she was doing, oblivious to the outside world. And she was happy. That much was clear to the man jealously watching her. She was happy as he'd never seen her in her life of luxury.

"Wait," he said softly, detaining Barnaby. "It would be better not to disturb her."

"That's what I said, ain't it?"

"You did indeed." He slipped a coin into Barnaby's thin hand. "Now take yourself off, there's a good fellow."

He stood in the shadows, watching as his wife moved from bed to bed. She wore the same gray dress as on the night when she'd appeared on his doorstep, bedraggled and desperate. He waited for her to notice him, but she had no attention for anyone but the ailing creatures to whom she was devoting herself.

But at last she did look up, and grew instantly still at the sight of her husband. There was shock on her face, but no pleasure, he noted, and she was frowning as she moved toward him. "How do you come to be here, Rupert?"

"I have come to take you home, my dear."

"I can't come now, I have too much to do," she said distractedly.

"Surely someone else can take over for you?"

"I gave my word." Her voice was gentle but implacable.

"Ah, yes," he said with a smile that was directed against himself. "Once before your given word deprived me of your company, didn't it? I will wait for you."

"There's no need. A hack will call for me in a couple of hours."

"In a couple of—a hack?"

"That's how I come here, and I arrange with the driver to call back later."

"You drive through streets like this on your own?" he demanded, outraged. "Have you any idea of the dangers?"

She drew in her breath sharply, and for a moment her eyes held an expression that he didn't understand. "Yes," she murmured. "I've learned the dangers. But I keep the blinds pulled down and Bill—he's my usual driver—is armed." A look of strain touched her face. "Rupert, please, let this be. My life here—"

"Is another of those things I wouldn't understand?"

"No," she said simply. "I don't think you would."

"Then you must explain it to me, my dear. For I am certainly going to remain."

Luckily Serena's arrival made further speech unnecessary. She was clutching the bank draft and was eager in her thanks. "This makes so much possible. My dear Lady Rupert, only look at the amount."

Calvina's eyes widened as she regarded the draft. Serena's shrewd gaze went from one to the other.

"I think you should go with your husband," she told Calvina. "I'll take your place here. I believe you have much to discuss."

"You might have told me, Calvina."

They were sitting in the carriage, on their way home. Calvina had been silent, sunk in gloom it seemed to her husband, and it was left to him to break the silence.

"There were reasons why I couldn't," she protested.

"When you asked me for money, it was for this, wasn't it?"

"They had to buy the building or be evicted."

"Yes, Miss Davison has explained. I had a most interesting talk with her, although I would rather have had it with you."

She was silent. He reached into his pocket, removed something, and slipped it into her hand. "It is not the first

137

time I've retrieved this for you. I think it should be the last."

Calvina gave a gasp of joy and pressed her lips to the brooch. "However did you find it?"

"Mrs. Andrews saw it in the pawnshop and 'felt it her duty' to inform me. That was when I learned of your repeated absences from home, and your refusal to tell anyone where you were going. You may imagine what construction the household put on that. It would have been kinder of you not to expose me to vulgar speculation."

"Yes, I'm sorry. I didn't think."

"Did you really have to pawn your brooch, rather than admit me into your confidence? You cannot have thought I would be displeased."

"No, not that. It's just that this is precious to me. It's the way I was raised. It makes me feel closer to Papa."

"And this dress? Why did you even keep it?"

"I'm not sure, except perhaps I wanted to remember who Calvina Bracewell was. Somehow I don't believe in her as Lady Rupert Glennister. So much luxury, when others have nothing, oppresses me."

"I'm beginning to comprehend a good deal. I still wish you'd told me everything, including why you slipped away from the masquerade. The rumors about you are disquieting, and it would have saved me much anxiety."

"What rumors?" she asked.

The startled innocence of her gaze brought it home to him how much he'd wronged her. The light had shifted, making his suspicions seem the ravings of a madman.

"What rumors?" Calvina repeated.

He colored, suddenly unwilling to reveal the baseness of his thoughts. "Nothing at all."

"You're not the man to be disquieted for nothing. What are people saying about me? Rupert, you must tell me."

"It's a trifle," he said with a shrug. "Ninian is convinced that you're about to present me with an heir, and I find this opinion is shared by much of society. Knowing you as I do I felt sure there must be another explanation."

"But not entirely sure," she said shrewdly. "What aroused your doubts?"

"When you deserted me at the masquerade, because you'd promised to meet someone else," he said, goaded. "I knew nothing about Trident House. What was I to believe?"

"You actually thought that I would—? So that was why you asked all those questions about Toby. You thought he'd fathered my child and I wanted your money to give to him. You actually believed—? *How dare you!*"

"Aren't you being a little unreasonable? If you'd been open with me—"

"You once said you trusted my father's daughter like no other woman. It's a pity you didn't hold to that, my lord."

"Don't start calling me 'my lord,'" he begged.

"I was overcome by the heat at Almack's, that is all, and so I told Ninian. Wait until I see him. I'll teach him to be a gabble monger."

"I am beginning to feel sorry for Ninian," Rupert observed dryly. "Now, can we abandon this subject and speak of something else? I've had much to say to you ever since a certain evening at Covent Garden, but was compelled to wait while your—er—other interests occupied you. Do me the justice to admit that I've been patient."

"And now I know what you thought my 'other interests' were," she seethed.

"Am I to blame for that, since you assured me that Toby Aylesbury was not in London?"

"And he is not."

"You are—shall we say—mistaken, my dear."

"Toby is here? But how? Why?"

"I don't know the details, but only yesterday I saw him with my own eyes."

139

Calvina took a deep breath. "I knew nothing of this. But you think I'm lying, don't you?"

"No, I don't think you're lying, and I apologize for my previous thoughts. You should ascribe it to the shock of seeing you look so different the other night. The wife I left behind never looked so, or behaved so. And you need not tell me that I shouldn't have left her behind, for I know it now. Why don't we take up where we left off that night? You see, I'm ready to make amends for my past neglect."

"For which, no doubt, I'm supposed to be grateful," she said, her spirit rising. "You finally condescend to remember my existence, but only after you've accused me of infidelity and trying to extort money from you by false pretenses—"

"I never—"

"And then you expect me to come running when you snap your fingers? Well, you were never more mistaken."

"Calvina—"

"I don't know what you imagined you were marrying, but if you thought me to be a spiritless ninnyhammer it's time I proved otherwise."

"We're nearly at home," he reminded her. "Quarrel with me if you like, but wait until we have some privacy."

"I have no wish to quarrel with you, my lord," she said with quelling formality. "My only wish is to bid you good night, and retire to my bedchamber—alone."

His face hardened. "In that case, madam, I will not impose my presence on you a moment longer." As soon as the carriage halted he handed her down with great ceremony, and escorted her to the front door. "Good night, madam."

"You mean—you're not coming inside?"

"For what purpose? You've already informed me of your own plans. It's early yet and the night still holds promise of diversions."

140

He waited until the porter had opened the door to admit her, gave her a curt bow, and returned to the carriage. Calvina heard him say, "Drive on!" Then the carriage moved off, leaving her staring after it, a prey to rage and disappointment in equal measure.

Sometimes Calvina wondered at the disturbance her husband caused her, when she still loved Toby. The memory of his gentleness and sweet nature could even now bring her pain. Rupert was neither gentle nor sweet-natured, but a man whose cool, ironical surface covered an inner explosiveness. Perhaps it covered much worse. She knew him to be arrogant, capable of ruthlessness, perhaps even cruelty, but did it go as far as actual wickedness? That was one of the many unanswered questions in the dark mystery that was her husband.

At the masquerade he'd said that soon she must yield to him, yet now he made no move to urge her, seemingly content with their game of cat and mouse. Sometimes she would glance up to find him watching her with a look in his dark eyes that made her blush all over. Again she would be tormented by the wanton thoughts that he alone could induce, and which made her confused. No truly virtuous woman would ever be troubled by such immodest ideas, let alone feel the blood pulse in her veins at the mention of his name.

And yet, with all this, she would fall asleep at night thinking of her lost love. Rupert had said Toby was in London, but their paths didn't cross, and at last she assumed he'd been mistaken, or deliberately tormenting her.

She couldn't ask him. Since the night of their quarrel he'd behaved as though nothing had happened between them. He remained in London, squiring her about with punctilious courtesy. He even drove her to Trident House and waited patiently until she was ready to leave. All London buzzed with the story of Lord Rupert's attentiveness toward his wife, and how a marriage of convenience seemed to be turning into a love match.

Only Calvina knew that the truth was even more curious. Her husband was watching, waiting for something. But surely, she thought, their moment had come with the masquerade? And then it had vanished. Yet he remained by her side. No matter how hard she tried to comprehend him, he had retreated into his mystery.

Then something happened that diverted her attention. A gilt-edged card arrived, inviting Lord and Lady Rupert Glennister to a ball at Ullaston House. Lady Ullaston followed it with a personal visit, to make certain that her "dear, dear friends" wouldn't fail her. Calvina had returned from a visit with her dressmaker to discover Lysandra closeted with Rupert. He greeted his wife warmly, but the next moment he was assuring Lysandra that they would certainly attend.

"Unless, of course, Lady Rupert prefers not to," Lysandra said archly.

Calvina would greatly have preferred not to, but there was no way that she could say no.

"My wife could have no possible reason for refusing," Rupert said firmly.

"I've sometimes had the sad feeling that I've incurred her dislike," Lysandra declared mournfully.

Civility forced Calvina to disclaim. It was settled that they would attend the ball, and Rupert showed Lysandra to her carriage. It seemed to her that he was gone an unnecessarily long time, and when he returned his first words were, "I wonder why she thinks you dislike her? You have no cause."

She longed to ask if this was really true, but he turned swiftly to another subject, and the words died.

Her gown for the ball was gold crepe over an underslip of yellow satin, trimmed with gold. She wore a diamond necklace, with matching bracelet and earrings. The set had been a recent gift from Rupert, and she knew she looked magnificent. She was a far cry from the gauche girl of her first meeting with Lysandra, and with a burst of confidence, she decided she had nothing to fear. She was smiling as she entered Ullaston House on Rupert's arm.

Nothing could have exceeded his attentiveness to his wife that evening, and when the dancing began he promptly offered her his arm.

"My lord, you surely don't intend to stand up with your wife?" Lysandra asked in a rallying tone. "Why, such a thing is shockingly dowdy."

"Oh, Calvina and I don't care for that," Rupert said with a grin. "We're an old married couple, deep in the delight of domestic life, aren't we, my dear?"

"Positively in the seer and yellow," Calvina responded. "I plan to ask my lord to give me a cat."

Nobody took this seriously, but the message that Lord and Lady Rupert were on excellent terms was clear. It even pierced the clouds of stupidity that shrouded Lysandra's brain. Her eyes narrowed and she brooded on the stratagem she'd planned for this evening. It seemed she was only just in time.

Smiling, Rupert led his wife onto the dance floor and they began the minuet. But the cordial understanding between them wasn't destined to last. All was well for the first few figures, but then Calvina saw something which shocked her.

Toby and Eglantine were dancing in the next set.

The sight startled her, so that she missed her footing and would have stumbled heavily had not Rupert caught her. "Are you unwell?" he asked at once.

"No, I—it's nothing—nothing."

She couldn't help stealing a glance in Toby's direction to see if he'd noticed her. His pale face told her that he had. Rupert saw everything and his eyes grew black.

"Perhaps the heat has overcome you," he said smoothly. "You would wish to retire."

"No," she said frantically. She knew it was unwise to betray her discomposure, but anything was better than leaving before she'd talked to Toby.

Eglantine was dancing with her husband. Three months of marriage had left her with a puffy face and a bloated figure. She was garishly dressed in acid yellow satin, a material ideally suited to emphasize her billowing curves. Around her neck she wore rubies.

She waved and called to Calvina, oblivious to the fact such behavior was bad ton. Calvina wondered at this show of friendliness, but when the dance was ended and Eglantine bustled over to her, with Toby in tow, it became clear that she wanted to gloat.

"La, cousin, fancy meeting you here," she gushed, according Calvina a relationship she'd never bestowed on her before. "I had thought ton parties were too worldly for you, but you're vastly improved. I must say, I'm not ashamed to know you."

"In—indeed," Calvina stammered, uncertain how to receive this piece of impertinence. "You've met my husband I believe?"

Rupert uttered silken courtesies that Eglantine received with all the flourishes of an acknowledged beauty. The effect was grotesque, and no one seemed to know it better than Toby, who flushed to the roots of his hair.

"I'm delighted to see you in London," Calvina said politely. "I had no notion you were coming."

"Oh, my lord and master insisted on it," Eglantine said, with a coy look at Toby. "He said that nothing but the best would do for me. I was simply obliged to yield."

"You're fortunate to have such a considerate husband," Rupert said smoothly.

"Indeed I'm the luckiest of women. He positively showers me with gifts." Eglantine fingered the rubies. "And he's so kind to dear Mama and Papa. I protested. I said to him, 'Master of my destiny, how can I so impose on your goodness as to let you care for my family?' But he brushed my scruples aside. 'Your family are mine,' he said, 'and what makes you happy, makes me happy.' "

"You are greatly to be felicitated," Rupert said with a small bow. "If you will excuse me, my hostess is trying to attract my attention." He strolled away.

Eglantine immediately burst into a paean of praise for Lord Rupert, conveniently forgetting that at their last meeting he'd thrashed her father. "I feared his reputation, as you know, cousin," she confided to Calvina. "But in London I find he's received in the first circles, so, of course, we couldn't refuse to know him."

"How kind of you," Calvina said gravely.

"My, you've grown so fine I hardly knew you. But I suppose anyone can be fine when they marry vast wealth."

"My dear," Toby protested quietly. "Your lively tongue carries you away."

"Oh, nobody cares for that in society," Eglantine said with a giggle. "Great ladies say whatever they like."

"Have you been very much in society?" Calvina asked, and if there was a touch of irony in her voice Eglantine could be relied on not to notice.

"Very little . . ." Toby began to say, but was drowned out by his wife.

"Oh lord, yes. We're invited everywhere. No party is complete without us. The Ullastons are our particular friends."

"We both wish to felicitate you on your marriage," Toby said to Calvina. "I hope very much that you are happy."

"It would be a strange thing if she wasn't happy, with all that money," Eglantine said sharply. "Indeed, I can't see why one little brooch was so—" She checked herself with a sharp hiss of breath and swiftly returned to her role of blissful young bride. "But not as happy as we are, Tobykins. I declare you've said a thousand times that no husband was ever so blessed."

Suppressing a wince at being called Tobykins, he said gently, "And meant it, my love."

"So there's no need for you to be so jealous all the time, you silly boy. I only flirt because it's the fashion, and the men simply insist on it. Oh look, here's Lord Ullaston. I daresay he wants the next dance. He's a dear old soul, and quite a beau of mine. Yoo-hoo!"

She tripped away, calling at the top of her voice. Lord Ullaston, who'd had no notion of her being there, hastily controlled his look of alarm, and allowed himself to be flirted with and dragged onto the dance floor. Calvina and Toby were left together. It was their first meeting since the night she'd fled the Dalrymples' home.

"I thought I would never see you again," he said painfully. "When I heard of your marriage I couldn't believe . . . but he must have forced you. For God's sake, say that it was not your choice!"

"I hardly know," Calvina answered slowly. "I ran to his house because there was nowhere else. I wanted to reproach him, but I was his wife before the night was out. Don't ask me how it happened." She gave a little sigh. "We have gone our different ways, Toby. What's done is done."

The waltz was beginning. Couples were already swirling past.

"Dance with me," he begged.

She knew it was unwise but her emotions were threatening to overwhelm her. To see him in such misery, and witness his generous forbearance toward his wife who shamed him, roused her love again. As in a dream, she went into his arms.

"I wish I hadn't come here," he said. "I've longed to see you again, but now it hurts too much."

"For me, too, but we mustn't talk about it. We're each married to other people. We must seem cheerful and speak of indifferent subjects."

He forced a smile. "It's good to see you looking so well, but quite unlike your old self."

"That's true. I've become a different person."

"But not in everything." He looked deep into her eyes.

"No, not in everything," she confessed in a low voice. "But you mustn't think of me, Toby. Everything is over for us."

"Don't say that. When I look at Eglantine—" He checked himself. "She is my wife," he said dully. "I owe her every loyalty. But oh, my darling, how am I to bear it?"

There was a painful lump in Calvina's throat. She turned her head away, frantically seeking some less dangerous topic. "I'm glad Eglantine is enjoying her season in London," she forced herself to say brightly at last. "It was a kindly thought of yours."

"It wasn't quite as she said," Toby responded grimly. "We never thought of London until Lady Ullaston's letter arrived, saying that she'd heard of us and would like to meet us. Eglantine was wild to accept, and to stay in town for several months. We arrived a month ago."

"And I haven't see you," she murmured.

"How should you? We have no friends, nobody asks us anywhere. This is our first invitation. I still don't understand how it all came about. I can't imagine where Lady Ullaston could have heard of us."

Calvina was silent. A monstrous suspicion was forming in her head. This was no accident. Lysandra had deliberately thrown her together with Toby. But how had she known of his existence, or where to write to him? Whatever the answer, Lysandra had deliberately tried to make trouble for her, and it seemed she'd succeeded. Rupert was waltzing with her, laughing at her sallies, and seemed delighted to be in her arms.

Lysandra was smiling up into her partner's face. "Confess it," she teased. "No one gives parties like I do."

"It's almost your greatest skill," he agreed.

"Almost? Come, tell me what my greatest skill is."

He grinned at her scandalously exposed breasts, and

she burst out laughing. "To be sure, there is that. And why not? You never complained."

"I never complain about generosity in a woman. Did you ever have to complain about lack of it in me?"

"Oh, money!" She made a face. "How trivial it is, after all!"

"You adopt a high tone, my pretty predator. I recall you in a different mood."

She pouted. "How ungallant of you!"

"Not at all. I simply prefer honesty. I take and I give. And then perhaps I take again. So runs the world."

"And what about your little puritan? Or *is* she such a puritan? Does she give in return for what she takes?"

His brow darkened. "We will not discuss my wife, if you please."

"Did she marry your fortune for love?" Lysandra persisted recklessly. "Or does she hanker after another lover, like the young man she's dancing with?"

His grip on her tightened in displeasure. "I warned you to stop this."

As they turned in the dance he could just make out Calvina and Toby, waltzing by, oblivious of all others. His sharp eyes noted their absorption in each other, the soft-voiced conversation that brought such a look of anguish to her face. His expression darkened into a glower. He'd given Calvina all his attention, delighting in her wit and honesty as much as her beauty. His reward was to be ignored while she danced with a callow boy who was unworthy of her. He didn't recognize the feeling as jealousy, never having known it before. He only knew that his wife was making a fool of him.

Calvina was full of confusion. How could she mind who was in Rupert's arms while she loved Toby? And yet she did. She minded passionately, even while her heart was aching as she said farewell to her true love.

"Dance the next one with me," Toby said urgently.

"We can never dance together again. You'll return to Bath soon . . ."

"If only I could," he groaned. "Eglantine is set on her family coming to London, so we'll be here awhile."

"Surely you don't have to do what the Dalrymples want?" she asked, puzzled by his failure to assert himself. "Just tell them your mind is made up."

"I keep meaning to do that, but when Hugh starts asking the Lord to forgive me for my hard-heartedness—"

"I know what he can be like. But I *had* to submit. You're a man. You can be firm."

He gave a helpless shrug, and she knew a stirring of dismay. She smothered it quickly. Toby wasn't weak. He simply had a gentle nature upon which others played.

"The dance will end soon," she whispered. "Good-bye, Toby."

"Good-bye, my darling . . . my darling . . ."

Calvina closed her eyes, drinking in his soft words. The next moment she felt herself brought to an abrupt halt. She heard a gasp from Toby, then Rupert's voice, as hard as iron.

"How fortunate that I was close enough to see my wife begin to faint," he said.

"I'm not fainting," Calvina began to say.

"I think you are, my dear," he interrupted her, but there was no affection in his tone. His eyes were black with rage. "I told you earlier I thought you were affected by the heat. We will leave at once."

Indignation at his high-handedness made her reply, "I've no wish to leave . . ."

"And I insist that you oblige me in this matter. To remain here *is not good for your health*." The glitter in his eyes was alarming.

"Lord Rupert," Toby said, "if you would allow me to—"

Rupert ignored him. "Are you coming with me, or are you not?" he demanded.

"Not while you're so unreasonable. For heaven's sake, my lord! Everyone is staring at us."

"They're about to stare a great deal more," he said grimly. Stooping, he lifted her up in his arms. "Now, madam, we are going home."

Chapter Nine

"How dare you—" she said frantically, as Rupert headed out of the ballroom, but her voice was drowned out by her husband's.

"My wife has fainted," he declared firmly. "Let me pass please."

He shouldered his way through the crowd. Furiously Calvina realized that she had no choice but to play her part. Protests and struggles would only be undignified. She allowed her head to droop against Rupert's shoulder. Through half-closed lashes she saw Lysandra's face full of baffled rage. However she'd meant her little trick to end, it wasn't like this.

When they were out of the ballroom she raised her head and stared at his profile. "You had no right to do that," she said angrily. "Let me down at once."

"I have every right to prevent my wife's shaming me in public."

"I did no such thing."

"Be silent," he said grimly. "I have things to say to you when we get home, but not here."

Her heart began to beat with apprehension. She'd seen her husband in many moods, but this black rage that came off him like a blast of ice was new to her.

He bore her straight to the waiting carriage and set her down inside. "Home!" he said curtly to the coachman, and got in, slamming the door after him.

"I will never forgive you for this," she said bitterly.

"How dare you create a scandal in the middle of a ballroom?"

"The scandal was yours, madam. I prevented matters getting worse, for which you should thank me."

"I danced with an old friend—"

"With a man whom you say you love," he corrected. "You've proclaimed that love to me, *to your husband*, on every possible occasion. I tolerated it when you knew how to behave, but tonight you went too far. You danced as though only he existed for you—"

"You are coarse and vulgar," she said, seething.

"Very well, I am coarse and vulgar. But I have the strangest aversion to a wife who lectures me about my low standards when her own conduct is shameless."

She tried to hurl an angry reply at him but he silenced her with a gesture. "We will say no more for the present. Wait until we're home, and then we can both speak our minds with some freedom. I assure you I have much to say."

"As have I," she informed him through gritted teeth.

Their arrival in Berkeley Square was a model of decorum. The porter bowed them through the door and watched with respectful approval as they mounted the stairs, her ladyship's hand resting decorously on her lord's arm.

But once Calvina had reached her bedroom, propriety gave way to furious indignation, which at first found release in tearing off her jewelry and hurling it onto the dressing table. She hadn't known that she had such a temper.

"I will never set foot out of this house in your company again," she declared. "You humiliated me in front of half of London—"

"Not nearly as much as you humiliated *me*, madam. You once said yourself that if you were no better than the others you were no use to me. I begin to think that's the truth. What is it about that milksop that your heart can't let him go?"

"I was saying good-bye to him," she cried. "That was our first meeting since I fled the Dalrymples."

"What a coincidence," he scoffed.

"It's no coincidence. He was specially invited to London by Lady Ullaston, with what purpose I leave you to imagine."

He stared. "What are you suggesting?"

"Lysandra arranged for him to be there, to make trouble between us."

"Nonsense, she knows nothing about him."

"She must. She wanted to make us quarrel, and she's succeeded. She's out to reclaim her property, and that's another thing that all London knows. Think of that before you speak of shameless conduct."

"I've never *belonged* to Lysandra or any other woman—"

"But you expect *me* to belong to *you*, don't you?"

"Oh yes, I expect that."

"And I never will. You'll simply have to accept it."

His eyes kindled. "Do you think you can make me accept it, Calvina?" He laid a hand on her neck. It was a gentle touch, but she could feel the iron strength in his fingers, and read the purpose in his eyes. The next instant he pulled her into his arms and his mouth was on hers in the fiercest kiss he had ever given her.

She tried to repel him, supported by her anger, but the most freezing rage couldn't help but thaw in the heat of the passion he evoked in her. She'd thought she could force herself to be indifferent to him, but the touch of his lips on hers stripped away that illusion. Her flesh would no longer be subdued to her will. It had a life of its own, and it wanted this man totally, shamelessly. Unable to do anything else, she returned his kiss with an urgency that matched his own. Her fingers curled in his hair, enjoying the sensuous feel of its springiness.

"I never accept what I don't like," he murmured against her lips. "You should know that by now. By God,

I've waited for you longer than any other woman, but now the waiting is at an end."

As he spoke he was pushing her dress from her shoulders. It slipped down easily, revealing her full, ripe breasts in all the glory of their nakedness. She gasped and would have tried to cover herself, but he instantly dropped his head and began to caress one proud nipple with his tongue.

The sensation was so shatteringly good that she moaned aloud. A fierce desire was welling up from deep within her body. So this was what people meant by carnal lust! It wasn't shocking or sinful at all. It was beautiful, and it could drive all else from the world, except the one man who could make her body sing.

The sheet was cool beneath her back as he laid her down on the bed and began to strip off his own clothes. She'd never seen a man's naked body before, but in the fever of her desire there was no time to be shocked. She was too innocent to know what was happening. She only knew that the throbbing between her legs was a part of it, and she was ready for the fulfillment that was beyond her comprehension.

He lay beside her and pressed her naked flesh against his own. Calvina could sense everything about him, the fever that raged in him and the moment when he leashed himself back and became mysteriously gentle.

"Don't be afraid of me," he said softly. "Come to me. Show me that you trust me."

Bewildered, she slipped her arms about his neck. She wasn't sure whether he moved over her of his own accord, or whether she pulled him over, but her legs seemed to part naturally to receive him. There was a shock, overtaken by a pleasure so intense that she felt she must die from it.

The moment she felt him moving inside her she began to move instinctively with him. Now she knew why her body had ached these last few weeks. It had wanted something she didn't understand. It had wanted *this*, and now that it had what it had yearned for, the craving was only increased.

"My lord . . ." she whispered.

"Hush, no words," he said with a smile. "No names. Only you and me."

In the new world to which he'd taken her, his meaning was instantly clear. The two of them existed outside time and space, and this joy was unlike anything else that had ever been. How had she lived twenty-four years without knowing that this was the real truth between men and women?

He still smiled, reassuring her that she was safe in his arms. Calvina cast aside the last shreds of caution and yielded herself up utterly to joy. She had thought that nothing could surpass the sensations that were coursing through her now, but she soon found that she was wrong. Rupert's movements became more vigorous, making her cry out with the fierceness of her pleasure. She was caught up in a spiral that twisted higher and higher. Above her she could see shinning pinnacles, whose beauty tempted her on. She reached for them and found that she was holding Rupert, clasping him close, molding her body to his.

She drew an expectant breath, longing for him to take her to those pinnacles, and when he did she was enveloped in light and white heat, clinging to him, seeing his face in the furnace. But it was all over in a blinding few moments.

"No," she cried. "Not yet!"

"We all want it to last forever," he whispered. "But it can never last. We must content ourselves with the promise of next time."

"Next time . . ." she echoed hazily.

"We have only started our journey," he promised. "It will be a glorious journey together, and we will find the bliss that passes all other delight. Sleep now."

*   *   *

She awoke in the early dawn to find Rupert, propped on his elbow, regarding her with a mixture of tenderness and irony.

"Well, madam?" he asked. "Did I do wrong to snatch you from the arms of Toby Aylesbury?"

For a split second she honestly couldn't think who he was talking about. The previous evening's events, and Toby himself, had retreated into the shadows. He saw her confusion and roared with laughter. He'd said once that in his arms she would forget Toby, and now she knew that he had been right. After a moment she joined in his laughter. He gathered her up and they clung together in an ecstasy of mirth, until his lips descended on hers, and laughter and everything else was forgotten in the next step of the journey. And it was as glorious as he had promised.

In the days that followed she found that her life had changed completely. All she wanted now was to be with Rupert, away from the demands of society. She longed to revel in his presence, night and day. He might not love her. He certainly never said so. But she knew that she pleased him, because there was a light in his eye that hadn't been there before. Perhaps if they were alone she might have a chance to win his love.

"Can't we return to the country for a while?" she asked one day.

"And leave the delights of London?" he teased. "Miss the rout parties, and Venetian breakfasts—"

"As though I cared for them!"

"Would you really like to spend some time at Glennister Court?"

"More than anything."

"Then we'll leave tomorrow."

"I'll visit Trident House today. Only—I've almost gone through my allowance, and—"

"And we're only halfway through the month," he finished with a grin. "Clearly I'm a nipfarthing, who's keeping you abominably short."

"Oh no," she protested. "But now the building is ours we're hoping to start a little school, and then—"

"Say no more," he told her, scribbling a draft on his bank. "Will that be enough?"

"More than enough," she said ecstatically.

He gave her a quizzical look. "Don't you ever want anything for yourself?"

She could have told him that she passionately wanted his love all for herself. But the light in his eye was teasing and ironical. It wasn't the moment. So she returned him a light answer and hurried away to get ready to go to Trident House. There she handed the money to Miss Davison, promised to return soon, and went home, dreaming of the joys of her new life.

Rupert drove her to Glennister Court in his curricle and four. It was high summer and the countryside was in bloom. Calvina thought she'd never seen anything so beautiful. Aunt Josie greeted her with open arms, and she felt that this place had now truly become her home for the first time.

Dinner was an endurance for them both. Josie had gone to much trouble to provide a superlative repast, and civility obliged them to try everything and pronounce it excellent. Then they must listen to her telling all the local gossip, and to Ninian with his more sober account of estate matters. But when their eyes met across the table each knew that the other was thinking only of the great four-poster bed in her room.

At last they were free, and in the hot, swirling darkness, with only themselves to please, they recaptured the passion that had brought them fulfillment, and found it more beautiful than ever.

Now it was obvious to Calvina that her love for Toby had been a dream born out of her loneliness. He was a weak boy, not to be compared with the strong man who'd possessed himself of her heart and her body. Now there was no one but Rupert in the world. Her love for him was total, abandoned, all consuming. She had not known that

157

such happiness existed. It seemed that life must continue forever on this beautiful plane, with nothing to worry about ever again.

The first time they went out riding Calvina begged for a more spirited horse. Rupert had heard of his wife's rapid advance as a horsewoman but demanded proof before he made a decision. One morning was enough to convince him, and the next day he presented her with Jenny, a beautiful mare, whose gentle appearance was belied by her lively eyes. Rupert watched her closely on their first gallop, but it was clear that Calvina had quickly established control. Jenny was spirited but sweet tempered, and they were soon on excellent terms.

Now she could ride beside him over the great Glennister estates. The tenants were eager to see her and showed her a mixture of warmth and curiosity. Toward Rupert they were more reserved, greeting him politely but with caution.

Wherever they went Calvina noticed the signs of a good landlord. In earlier days she'd frequently made parish visits to farmworkers who lived in squalor that would have disgraced pigs, because their landlords grudged money for repairs. Rupert's tenants were housed well, their repairs done regularly. There were also several charitable schemes in place, and even a school for the children of his workers.

She guessed that Ninian was the instigator, but she knew that he could have done nothing unless Rupert supplied the money. The tenants must know it, too, which made their nervousness strange, unless they also believed the demonic rumors.

It was the blacksmith's wife who told her the most curious story. Calvina had called on Mrs. Arkright while Rupert refreshed himself at the nearby tavern. The two women drank tea in the garden together, interrupted by Mrs. Arkright's repeated admonitions to her sons to stop wrestling and behave themselves.

158

"Mickey will keep setting on his brothers." She sighed. "But there, when I think that he was dead, I can't be hard on him."

"Dead?" Calvina echoed in astonishment.

"Dead as a stone, your ladyship!" Mrs. Arkright declared, almost with an air of triumph.

"But he's *not* dead."

"He was, once. Such a terrible fall he took, and lying there, dead and cold. But his lordship said a spell over him, and Mickey came back to life."

"But that's impossible. Mickey *can't* have been dead—"

"The doctor said he was as dead as dead," Mrs. Arkright declared firmly. "But his lordship told him to stand aside, while he made an incantation over him. Suddenly there were great clouds of smoke, and the air was filled with the smell of sulfur. His lordship lifted him up and said he was alive now, and under his special protection. Then he waved a hand, and the smoke vanished in a trice."

Calvina made some indifferent answer, but she was shaken. Whatever the truth, Rupert must have performed an act of benevolence, but in such a way that it had seemed demonic. Indeed, it was hard to see how he could have raised the dead, unless . . .

"What ails you?" he asked as they rode home. "You've been silent for an hour."

"You'll think me foolish," she said slowly. "The story must be nonsense, of course, but she seemed so certain."

"You've been talking to Mother Arkright. Has she told you I brought her son back to life?"

His amused tone calmed her and enabled her to say lightly, "With spells and incantations, no less."

Rupert threw back his head and laughed so loudly that the birds in the trees above took offense and scattered, twittering.

"Spells and incantations!" he echoed at last. "I'll swear

the tale grows every time she tells it. Did I turn into a crow and fly away?"

"No, you restored the boy to life, and said he was under your special protection."

"You mean the devil's special protection, don't you? I'm very sure that's what *she* meant." He grinned at her. "I'm sorry if it disappoints you, but, as you've always suspected, I'm not the devil. Just an ordinary sinner."

His humor vanished suddenly, and he frowned. "When I was a boy I made the mistake of admiring my father. I was too young to understand that he really was evil, and he broke my mother's heart. He was only ever interested in me when I got into some scrape. It became a way of getting his attention. By the time I knew better I'd discovered that I enjoyed kicking up larks and shocking my neighbors.

"I made friends with the village doctor. He was a kindly soul who saw through my wicked aura to the confused boy I was underneath. He taught me a lot. But then he died, and Doctor Edwards, the man who replaced him, was a fool.

"Mickey Arkright was never dead. The fall knocked him out and he stopped breathing. Luckily, I chanced to be on hand, and remembered what the old doctor had taught me. I managed to start him breathing again by rubbing his chest. Edwards, of course, had already pronounced him dead, and couldn't say otherwise without revealing his ignorance.

"To the villagers it seemed confirmation that I had supernatural powers. Even the child's mother crossed herself as soon as she'd thanked me."

"How stupid and unkind!" Calvina said indignantly.

"I didn't think so. I had a sense of power over them, and I was sufficiently young and foolish to enjoy that. Since then the story's been told and retold, with ever more lurid details added. I've enjoyed the fun, but it's time it stopped now." His eyes were warm and amused.

160

"Don't believe the worst of me, my—" He checked himself and she wondered hopefully what he meant to call her. But he continued, "I can't have my wife deluded by such tales."

It was often that way. She could feel them drawing closer to each other, and he would pause on the edge of an endearment. Then caution seemed to overtake him, and he would turn the matter aside with a light remark. It was disappointing, but she was too happy to dwell on it.

If his heart was still a mystery, his mind at least was opening to her. Now he had time to show her around his laboratory and demonstrate the concoctions that he made, which were mostly herbal remedies, taught him by his doctor friend. He had shelves laden with small bottles made of blue glass, each one neatly labeled.

"Just medicines, you see," he said with a grin. "My tenants come to me for them, and I do them less harm than Doctor Edward's quackery."

"They think you're the devil, and yet they still come to you for medicine?"

"Strange, isn't it? They know my potions are good. That's why they come. Yet they still cross themselves as they scurry away."

Once she dared to ask him about the duel Ninian had described to her, and he merely laughed. "My dear girl, who do you imagine alerted the magistrates?"

"Well—I've always thought that Ninian did."

"Did he say so?"

"No, but when he said that no one knew who it was—"

"Of course. I couldn't have it publicly known. I should never have accepted that child's challenge, but I was in a rage. Having gotten embroiled I had to find a way out, without backing down. Don't remind me of it. It's not one of the shining episodes of my life."

Day followed blissful day, with the two of them riding out alone, happy simply to be in each other's company. Together they visited the small Belmont estate that Rupert had been trying to sell.

"I nearly had a buyer recently," he confided as they looked over the comfortable house, "but he backed off at the last moment. The sooner I'm rid of the place the better."

"It doesn't hold any memories for you then?' she asked.

"None at all. My father only bought it to prevent a wealthy merchant living too close to him. Then he added injury to insult by letting it stand empty. I'm not so toplofty. I've had it put into good repair, but a house only flourishes when it's lived in. I'll sell Belmont to anyone rather than see it go to waste."

As they rode home in the twilight Calvina remarked, "It's time we looked out for a suitable wife for Ninian."

He grinned. "Can no female wed without becoming a matchmaker for all her friends?"

"If she's happy in her marriage," Calvina said hesitantly, meeting his eye.

"And are you happy in your marriage, my provoking witch?"

"Ask me first thing tomorrow morning," she responded demurely, which made him laugh.

"Has Ninian never shown a *tendre* for any female?" she resumed after a moment.

"I recall a few calf loves, which passed easily. Unfortunately fathers tend to think him ineligible for their daughters. He's my heir, of course, but who's to say that I'll die in time to turn him into a good match?"

"Poor Ninian," Calvina said. "He works so hard here and gains nothing himself."

"I pay him handsomely."

"But if he had an establishment, would he not be better situated than he is now?"

Their eyes met, and the same thought came to each of them. "Belmont!" Rupert exclaimed. "If I give him Belmont it will go some way to recompense him. Why didn't I think of it before?" He looked at her suddenly.

162

"Perhaps because I didn't have you to put clever ideas into my head."

"Rupert, I swear I only just thought of this," she protested. "I'm not a managing female . . ."

"Don't put yourself into a fret. I believe you. It's the effect you have, without saying or doing anything."

He spoke lightly, but there was a warmth in his smile that filled her with happiness. If only, she thought, he would say that he loved her. Only then could she tell him how much she loved him.

By the next day he'd thrown an army of servants into the house. Calvina supervised the cleaning, and even did some polishing herself, which made the servants stare. There was murmured grumbling when she brought a triumphant gleam to a tabletop that everyone else had given up, and quietly made it clear that this was the standard she expected. But nobody dared to speak openly. They'd seen their master's caressing gaze follow his wife, and were taking bets on how long his volatile interest would last.

There was an awkward moment when Ninian came riding by and caught her in an apron with a smudge on her cheek.

"Has Rupert put you to work?" he asked, grinning.

"To be honest, this is what I enjoy," she confessed. "There's something about getting a good shine on furniture that satisfies me like nothing else. Although I suppose it's bad ton to say so."

"What a strange wife you are for a man with Rupert's habits. You'd have made an admirable helpmeet for a man living on a mere competence. As it is, I fear your skills may be wasted."

"Not at all," she said merrily. "Rupert needs my skills as much as a poor man. He's giving generous support to a pauper house in town."

"Your doing, I collect. I thank God your influence on him is so good."

163

"And yours. I've seen for myself that he's an excellent landlord."

"He is, isn't he?" Ninian agreed quickly. "The impulse comes from him, you know. I merely carry out his ideas. But he's left me in ignorance about this house. I collect he's making another push to sell it."

"I believe so," Calvina said blandly. She was thinking of his delighted surprise when he learned the truth, but as he galloped away she couldn't help frowning. Something in Ninian's manner troubled her. She liked him for his eagerness to think the best of Rupert, but it seemed to her that his praise of his cousin had been slightly forced. The next moment she forgot him in the hurry to be finished.

At last the house smelled deliciously of wax polish and the flowers with which Calvina had filled it. Rupert and Calvina spent much trouble over the wording of the message that summoned Ninian to be present.

"Slightly curt, I think," Rupert mused. "So that he doesn't suspect it's anything but business."

Aunt Josie, who was in on the secret, joined them at Belmont, to await Ninian's arrival, and she was the first to see him through the window. Rupert continued his curt manner until the last moment, handing Ninian papers that would "explain everything," and standing back for the result. When it came it was all anyone had hoped.

"But—these are title deeds," Ninian stammered. "Bearing my name."

"Which should have been there long since," Rupert declared heartily, shaking him by the hand. "Welcome to your property."

To everyone's delight an expression of awed joy came over Ninian's face, but not until Josie and Calvina had hugged him thoroughly did he seem to believe in his good fortune. Then they all looked at the plans of the estate to see the farms it included, and how many tenants Ninian had. It was but a speck beside the glories of Glennister Court, but it made Ninian a man of property.

"Does this mean you wish to find another agent?" he asked, a little troubled.

"Certainly not," Rupert responded at once. "I couldn't do without you. But Belmont is your independence. When we quarrel you'll be able to walk out on me."

"Us quarrel?" Ninian asked fervently. Rupert clapped him on the shoulder. Nothing more needed saying.

"So this was why you worked to set the place in order," Ninian said as Calvina showed him the house, pointing out all the little touches she'd added for his comfort. "This was your doing, wasn't it?"

"Not at all. Rupert and I had the idea together."

"But you put it into his head. He told me this should have happened sooner. But it never could have happened without you."

"How can you say that when you know how much Rupert values you?"

"Not enough to show it before. You don't know what it means to me to know that I hold a little place in your heart."

Pitying his loneliness, she touched his arm, saying, "More than a little place. After Rupert, you're my dearest friend."

He gave a curious little laugh. "Is that really what you think Rupert is? Your friend?"

"No," she said gently. "Much more than a friend."

"That's not what I—Calvina, have you ever thought that if only you and I had met first—"

Her eyes widened. "Ninian, don't say such things."

He made a grimace of pain. "Of course not! I know my place. Loyal Ninian, the poor cousin who thinks of nothing but Rupert's interests, because he has none of his own—"

"But you have now," she reminded him.

"Oh yes, a crumb from his plate, prompted by you. But Ninian will still put his master first and himself second. Do you ever think how much of a strain that can be? Especially when the one woman I could have—"

165

"Please stop this!" she said urgently. "You don't mean it. You know you don't."

"Why are you so sure I don't?" he demanded with soft vehemence. "Because loyal Ninian will always smother his own feelings? Therefore he can't *have* any feelings. He can't love, and if he does, he wouldn't dream of telling her because—" He stopped himself with a shudder and passed a hand over his eyes. "My God, what am I saying? I never meant to speak these thoughts, but to conceal them forever. It's only that you—your kindness, your tenderness—" He seemed on the verge of tears.

"But we are all good friends, are we not?" she asked, eager to restore the relationship to its previous footing.

"Yes, of course." He gave a bitter laugh. "We're all good friends. I won't forget that again. Just let me have the joy of knowing that I once told you of my love, and that I long to serve you. I'll ask for no more, if you'll promise to turn to me when you need—a friend."

"More than a friend," she said fervently. "My dearest brother. I'll turn to you before anyone."

"What happened today will never happen again. It was a moment's weakness, no more." He closed his eyes, as if in despair.

"It didn't happen," she assured him.

"Will you tell Rupert?"

"How can I tell him something that didn't happen?"

He whispered, "God bless you for your generous heart," and hurried away, leaving her with tears of pity in her eyes.

She dried them firmly before Rupert saw her again. Not for the world would she have risked a breach between the two men by repeating Ninian's wild words. She tried to believe he couldn't have meant them, and her earnest hope was that he would find a wife who would drive herself from his heart. When she was sure she could present a bright face to the world she went downstairs.

*   *   *

It was Rupert's habit to ride out alone in the early morning. Sated from a night of loving, Calvina would kiss him sleepily good-bye and doze off again until the maid brought her morning chocolate.

One morning, he said, "I wonder why you never choose to accompany me."

"I do choose," she protested. "But I thought it pleased you to have some time alone."

He kissed her lightly. "It pleases me more to have your company. Hurry now."

Delighted, she quickly donned her deep blue riding habit, and together they went down to the stables. Rupert had sent on a message to have Jenny saddled, and all was ready for them.

A soft mist was rising from the land as they rode. Dawn had just broken, and wherever they looked trees were emerging into the hazy light. Calvina breathed in the cool air joyfully. With her senses roused by Rupert's passion, she seemed to have come alive to a thousand new sensations that had once passed her by. Her whole body reacted to the beauty of the morning, the feel of Jenny beneath her, moving rhythmically, and above all, the nearness of the man she loved. She admired his broad shoulders beneath his claret-colored coat and the way his tight-fitting buckskin breeches and high boots accented the strong muscles of his legs.

Suddenly he increased his speed, she followed him, and soon they were galloping like the wind, soaring over hedges and ditches together. She laughed aloud with exhilaration. The gallop left them both hungry, and at last they turned with one movement and headed for home, although at a slower pace.

On the way Rupert began to speak of Ninian, and the gift of Belmont. He seemed anxious to be reassured that his cousin was now happy.

"Can you doubt it?" Calvina asked. "He loves Belmont. Look at how much time he spends there."

"True. He's almost given up his rooms at home, preferring to sleep in his own house and join us in the morning. I shouldn't have waited so long to do this. I fear he may have labored under a sense of injustice."

"Better late than never," Calvina reminded him.

"True. At least now he may be—content."

There was an odd note in his voice. Calvina was about to ask what he meant when his head went up sharply. "What was that?"

He reined in his horse, alert. Calvina had halted beside him, and sat listening intently.

"Over there," Rupert said, frowning.

She followed his pointing finger and this time she heard the sound of gunfire. It was faint and seemed to come from a clump of trees on their left.

"Poachers!" Rupert said grimly. "Wait here."

He moved as if to start his horse, but Calvina seized his arm. "Rupert, let them go," she implored.

"Ignore poachers destroying my young game?" he demanded in astonishment.

"Don't hand them over to the constable," she said frantically. "They can be transported, or even hanged. If only you knew—I've seen such terrible things—"

"What should be done with criminals?" he asked, watching her intently.

"But most of them aren't criminals," she cried wildly. "Just poor people who poach for food. Why should we claim so much when they have so little? Rupert, I beg you, let them go."

"Calm yourself," he said after a moment. "I shan't hand them over. But I must drive them off."

"Couldn't you just pretend we'd heard nothing?"

"If I don't give them a fright they'll come back, and next time it may be one of my gamekeepers who surprises them. He *would* hand them over to the law, before I knew about it."

"Oh yes, you must prevent that," she agreed.

"Stay here," he ordered. "If they have guns I don't want you near."

"But you—" she protested, still holding his arm.

He smiled grimly. "Don't worry. No poacher will aim at me, for fear of my 'evil eye.' "

He galloped off. Calvina watched him until he was out of sight. The light was growing brighter every moment, but suddenly she shivered. How many times had wretched families appealed to her father to save one of their members from a dreadful fate! A compassionate man, he had always striven to mitigate the sentence, but it was hard, dispiriting work. His own kinsman, Lord Stoneham, had unhesitatingly prosecuted all poachers, and had once written to Calvin Bracewell, demanding that he cease his efforts, as they implied a criticism of his noble relative. That was the only notice the Stonehams had ever taken of them.

Calvina strained her ears for the sound of voices in the little copse, but she could hear none. All about her the birds were awakening, singing their dawn chorus. It was the start of a beautiful day, yet she felt as if a weight were oppressing her. She wasn't a fanciful woman, but at this moment she could almost believe that behind the soft light of a summer dawn lurked something evil.

Suddenly she heard the sound of a gun, very loud. In the next split second something whistled past her cheek, clipping Jenny on the ear and making her rear up. Calvina fought to keep her seat but the terrified animal plunged and kicked wildly until she was hurled over its head. She landed hard and felt the wind knocked out of her. The next few moments were terrible as she fought for breath, whooping and wheezing frantically, while Jenny seized her chance to escape.

At last Calvina regained her breath and struggled back to her feet, annoyed with herself for having let go of the rein. She looked around cautiously, but now there was only silence. One of the poachers must have fired and immediately taken fright. She called Jenny, but the horse had completely vanished.

Without warning a second shot rang out close to her. She just managed to fling herself down before the third bullet was fired.

"Rupert!" she screamed, flattening herself as much as she could.

There was no sound but the birdsong, continuing as though nothing had blasted the beauty of the morning. Her limbs seemed to have turned to lead, and she could do nothing but lie on the ground, wondering what would happen next.

At last she heard the sound she'd longed for, hoofbeats approaching fast, and Rupert's voice calling desperately, "Calvina! *Calvina!*"

He threw himself down beside her, cradling her in his arms and raising her from the ground. His face had a dreadful pallor. "Are you hurt?" he demanded. "Tell me, *are you hurt*?"

"No," she said with a gasp.

"Are you sure? When I saw your horse galloping away, and then you, lying on the ground—" He closed his eyes.

"I was just scared—they fired at me three times—"

"The poachers you were so eager to protect tried to kill you."

"You saw them?"

"No, the copse was empty when I got there. I saw no one. But by God, I'll find out who did this and—" He held her close, almost making her breathless again. But she didn't mind. It meant everything to her to know that Rupert was distraught at her danger. She put an arm about his neck as he lifted her to her feet.

"Jenny will be halfway home by now," he observed. "We'll go back together."

Gently he lifted her onto his horse and mounted behind her. She rested against him contentedly. She felt she could have gone on like this forever, held against his heart, but all too soon they saw men on horseback approaching them. Jenny had reached the house, and a team of grooms had set out instantly to find Calvina. They let out shouts of relief when they saw their master and mistress unhurt.

Rupert gave them terse instructions to pursue the poachers, dispatched one of them for a doctor, and spurred on home.

The doctor confirmed that there were no injuries but recommended his patient should rest for at least a day. This Calvina resolutely refused to do. Aunt Josie, entering a few minutes later, found her dressing and deaf to all protests. Even Josie's appeal to Rupert to exercise his husbandly authority failed to have the desired effect.

"I'm strong and healthy," Calvina told him firmly, "and I won't coddle myself merely because I've been alarmed."

"And suppose I order you, as your husband?"

"Don't," she said simply.

He grinned. "All right. I won't try where I'd be sure to fail. Let me help you fasten that dress."

"Do you know how to fasten a lady's dress?"

"Come, Calvina, you know my reputation."

"I do, and I take leave to tell you, my lord, that no gentleman would make such a remark to his wife."

"What a good thing I married you," he said, amused. "So many things I didn't know until you told me."

"Is there any news of the men who shot at me?"

"None, so far. But they'll be caught. They can't have gotten far."

"If it *was* poachers," she mused.

"My dear, what else could it be?"

"Rupert, there's something I should have told you before. This isn't the first time someone has tried to do me harm."

171

Briefly she described how she'd been forced to jump from the speeding hack.

"Why the devil didn't you tell me about this before?" he demanded.

"I longed to—at least, at first. But I hadn't told you of my visits to Trident House—I meant to tell you everything that night, but you looked so angry. I know now what you were thinking."

"I wonder if you do," he returned with a touch of grimness.

"You were thinking about Toby, weren't you? In fact, you looked astonished to see me, which isn't surprising if you thought I was with him."

"I don't know what I thought. I trusted you, but you were dashed secretive—no matter. We'll speak of that another time. Are you sure the driver was deliberately trying to harm you, and that the horses didn't simply bolt?"

"I thought of that, but I heard him urge them on. And he wasn't my usual driver, but one who presented himself an hour early."

"There's no significance in that. Your visits to Trident House must have been common knowledge among the drivers by then. Doubtless one of them tried to poach a good customer. If he really did urge on his horses, he must have been trying to impress you with his speed, but I think you imagined that part."

"But—"

"My dear, the notion that anyone would deliberately set out to injure you is too fantastic to be believed. The men who fired those shots today will soon be apprehended, and found to be poachers who simply took fright. In the meantime, I recommend that you forget the whole matter."

His manner was so reassuring that Calvina was glad to do as he suggested. Since autumn was approaching they departed for London a week later. Calvina plunged into purchasing a new wardrobe for the coming season and was too much occupied to worry about the fact that the poachers had not been caught, and all attempts to discover their identities had been fruitless.

Chapter Ten

For a few weeks London had been thin of company, as much of the ton followed the Prince Regent to Brighton, where he held sway at the Pavilion, his fantastic seaside palace. But now they were flocking back again, ready to plunge into another round of gaiety.

Among the many cards on the Glennisters' mantelpiece was one from Lady Covington, inviting them to attend a masquerade to be held in her home in Grosvenor Square. It was probably the last outdoor party before the weather grew chilly, and Rupert was at one with Calvina in wishing to accept. But two days before, he suddenly announced that he must return to Bath.

"Can't I go with you?" she asked longingly.

He kissed her swiftly on the mouth. "Not this time. I mean to look into a certain matter—you will be better off here."

Though their passion was as intense as ever they still behaved by day with civility and sometimes a certain distance, as befitted a married couple. Calvina longed to ask her husband about a constraint that had recently appeared in his manner, but she was cautious about plaguing him with questions. Now she thought of it, he'd frowned a good deal since they'd returned to London. It hurt a little that he hid his thoughts, and to the last moment she hoped that he would confide in her. But he departed without doing so, advising her to enjoy the masquerade.

Far from enjoying it Calvina would have cried off, but for the Hadden twins. George's courtship of Miss

Grandham proceeded by fits and starts. The lady was inclined to favor him, but her parents preferred the viscount.

"I plan to show her the Covington maze," George explained with a significant look.

"Miss Grandham has very strict notions of propriety," Calvina protested. "She will never consent to visit the maze alone with you."

"But she will if you're there as chaperon."

"George, I won't be a party to luring Miss Grandham into your company and leaving you alone."

"Of course not," he said, shocked. "You'll be there all the time."

She had meant to don the gown she'd worn for the Ullastons' ball, but Prudence informed her firmly that this wouldn't do. Unless she wanted to be thought a dowdy it was her duty to order a new dress and domino.

In the end she purchased a dress of silver gauze, trimmed with floss silk. The underslip was very pale yellow, and over these she wore a domino of deep rose silk. Her mask was the same rose color, heavily spangled.

The festivities took place out-of-doors. There was a supper room inside for the older guests, and a card room for the gentlemen. But the real interest was in the Covingtons' magnificent grounds, with their elaborate maze, and splendid ruin.

George was on the alert for Miss Grandham's arrival, and Simon had a quarry of his own to pursue. His father had urged an excellent alliance on him. Horrified, Simon had resisted. He'd never met Lady Ann Stanhope, but the more her virtues were described, the more averse to her he became, and he avoided all chance of meeting her. Calvina, determined to promote the match, had invited him to her rout party, promising him that Lady Ann would not be present. She then shamelessly broke her word, for which she felt heaven would forgive her. The result was all she'd hoped. The lady was a dazzling beauty, and Simon had promptly embarked on a campaign to recover lost ground.

For some time the three of them admired the gardens, which were enchanting. Fairy lamps hung from the trees, and highly colored dominoes flitted in and out of the shadows, chasing and being chased. Soft, teasing laughter could be heard from every glade, and the maze was put to good use as nymphs and satyrs flirted and darted down alleyways.

At last the twins drifted away in search of their inamoratas. Calvina felt no resentment at being thus abandoned. Love was a serious business, and she only hoped they would find happiness in marriage, as she had.

Despite the masks, she had no trouble recognizing Lady Ullaston. Her gold domino was thrown back revealing her ample charms sheathed in a red-satin gown, trimmed with gold, which was scandalously low cut, even for an informal occasion. The man on her arm was a spindly fellow, of no consequence. Certainly it wasn't Rupert, but Calvina hadn't expected it to be. Rupert was hers now, and her confidence had grown so much that she was able to greet Lysandra amiably.

Lady Wilmington, sitting in a little arbor with her bosom bow, Lady Dernish, remarked acidly, "I wonder that she's here tonight at all. They say Ullaston can't last long."

"Sinking by the hour, I heard," her friend replied.

Mr. Simmington had joined them. He was dressed only as himself, having positively refused to wear a mask and domino. Now he produced a purple snuff box that exactly matched his coat, sniffed delicately, and declared, "That's why she's here. She'll have to go into deep mourning soon, and she's enjoying herself while she can."

Lady Dernish gave a snort. "Deep mourning! That creature."

"But, my dear ma'am, of *course*!" Simmington exclaimed. "Think of the new dresses that will have to be

176

ordered, the black silk and satin, black velvet, black beads, fans, veils. Her white skin and red hair will look ravishing against black. What a widow she'll make! It's all too, too affecting." He wiped his eye.

"She'll be lucky if Ullaston's family allows her to spend so much as a groat," Lady Wilmington declared. "They've gathered in the house, you know, ready to heave her out-of-doors the moment he's gone."

"More fool her to have come to a masquerade!" Lady Wilmington said. "She should have stayed at home, protecting her position."

"But what can she do?" Mr. Simmington asked plaintively. "They say James has already taken charge of his father's desk, and refuses to let Lysandra in the room, while he goes through the papers. No, no, she's much better occupied in snaring the next husband."

A sudden silence fell on the little group, and all eyes turned to Calvina, who'd appeared through the trees. There was no knowing how much she'd heard, but her unmasked face was pale.

"Calvina," Mr. Simmington said, rising and kissing her hand, "I positively must drink champagne with you. The ladies will excuse us, I'm sure." He swept Calvina off on his arm.

"I know where the best champagne is to be had," he confided. "They've set up a charming little table, decked with vine leaves, just past that incredibly vulgar Greek statue. Pure fake, of course . . ."

He rattled on until Calvina stopped him by saying firmly, "They're all thinking of Rupert, aren't they? But they're wrong. It isn't true—at least not now."

"But, my dear, of course."

"If Lysandra Ullaston has come here looking for Rupert, she's wasting her time. He isn't even at this masquerade."

"Isn't—?" For a moment he looked startled.

"He had to return to Bath unexpectedly. You saw me arrive. Did you see Rupert with me?"

177

"No," he said gravely. "I didn't see Rupert arrive with you."

The twins returned in company with their ladies. Mr. Simmington, finding himself no longer the center of attention, drifted away.

"I was telling Miss Grandham how eager you were to see the maze," George said ingenuously.

"My evening would be quite ruined if I didn't see the maze," Calvina responded with a twinkle in her eye.

George proposed that they should form a party. Simon and Lady Ann declined to join them. Lord Stanhope had appeared in the distance, and Simon had much to say to him. From Lady Ann's shining eyes there could be no doubt of the subject.

The other three made their way into the maze. Calvina kept a strict eye on George, but it soon became apparent that Miss Grandham was no unwilling damsel, and would gladly have dispensed with a chaperon. It took her only a few moments to do so, darting away down an alley with George, and vanishing between the hedges. Calvina searched in vain before concluding that it was useless to search for two people who were determined not to be found, and made her way back to the entrance.

The maze stood apart from the rest of the gardens, surrounded by trees. Calvina could still see the lights and hear the laughter, and she'd begun to make her way toward them when a figure appeared in the shadows. He was a very large man, completely enveloped in his domino. She turned away, but he hurried after her.

"Not so fast," he called, detaining her with a hand on her arm. "Stay and entertain me for a while."

"I have no wish to entertain you," Calvina said firmly. "I don't know you."

"If only you did," the man said. "We could have such a nice time."

"Nor do I want a nice time with you," Calvina snapped. "Please take your hand away."

He giggled, regaling her with brandy fumes. "Naughty

178

lady to play games with me. I wonder what you're doing here alone? Is your lover late? Never mind. I'm here."

Furiously Calvina pulled herself free and began to run. He lumbered after her, moving slowly because of his bulk. She had reached the lights before he caught up.

"Oh, you're a coy little thing!" he caroled. "Never mind. I like 'em that way." He tried to draw her close for a kiss, but she struggled madly and managed to tear his domino badly. He swore and redoubled his efforts, groping for her mask until it slipped off, whereupon Calvina boxed his ears so soundly that he yelped. Now his mask, too, was awry. He made a frantic grab for it, but she snatched it and tossed it away. The next moment she was staring at his face in sheer disbelief.

"Hugh!" she gasped.

In the stunned silence that followed, Hugh's domino gave up the effort to hang together and slithered to the ground, revealing him in a pink-satin, swallow-tailed coat, and matching knee breeches, both heavily spangled. The lights winked off the spangles, emphasizing every line of Hugh in all his fat glory. Calvina took a deep, astounded breath.

"How came you to be in a place like this?" she asked at last.

But Hugh was equal to the situation. It was true that he gobbled like a turkey cock, but only for a moment.

"How came I?" he echoed indignantly. "How came *you*? That I should see the young woman I cherished as one of my own family flaunting herself at what I can only call an orgy! I have beheld things tonight it would shame me to speak of."

"If your behavior to me is any guide, you've *done* a few things it would shame you to speak of," she retorted indignantly.

Hugh threw his arms to heaven. "Strike me, insult me, abase me!" he cried. "I endure it all. The world's scorn is a small price to pay for the work of the Lord."

"Fiddlesticks!" Calvina snapped.

179

"Ah, you do not believe the Lord sent me here."

"I'm sure the Lord never told you to wear that ridiculous costume, which is suited to neither your age nor your figure."

"There's nothing wrong with my figure," he spluttered. "I'm in the prime of life. Several ladies have—that is—"

"Quite!" Calvina said coolly. She was wondering how she could ever have been alarmed by this clown.

"You don't understand," Hugh said urgently. "Things aren't what they seem. I am doing missionary work."

"Really, Hugh!"

"No, it's true, it's true. When my dear son-in-law implored me to visit with him and Eglantine, I accepted because I felt I should broaden my experience of life, the better to perform my great work. I expected to find London a circle of hell, and that's what I did find."

"Then you should have immediately returned to Bath."

"Not so. I realized that it was my duty to stay and help these poor fallen creatures. For this, I must understand their lives and the temptations to which they are exposed. Ah, if you knew the pain it has cost me, the trials I've undergone! I forced myself to come to this dreadful place and pass among the throng, incognito."

"And steal a few kisses, incognito." Calvina was beginning to be entertained.

"How the heathen misjudge the godly man! I merely pretended to make advances in order to sort the sheep from the goats. If a woman repulsed me I gave fervent thanks for her virtue. I was testing you, just now. If you'd yielded I would have prayed for your salvation."

"Indeed? And how far would you have taken the experiment before breaking off and starting to pray?"

He drew himself up. "This is a most improper conversation. Under my roof such thoughts would never have entered your head."

"Under your roof I never saw you bursting out of pink-satin breeches."

"Will you leave my shape out of this?"

"Suppose I was to tell your wife how you've been behaving?"

"I pray that you will, that my treasure may share my glory. She, too, is offering spiritual food to the heathen."

"You don't mean she's here?"

"Naturally. Our great work is achieved together. With my own eyes I've seen that noble woman attempting to entice a young man with her charms. I am happy to say that he found the strength to resist."

Calvina didn't think she could stand much more of this. Her face ached from the effort to keep it straight.

"And what about your mother?" she asked. "Is she—er—doing missionary work as well?"

"She tried. I saw her set out in a blue-satin cloak and diamond eardrops to show these sinners the error of their ways. Alas, the spirit was willing but the flesh was weak. Rheumatism, you know. She is now recruiting her strength with a little light supper."

"I think we should join her," Calvina said firmly.

She led the way through the grounds to the supper rooms. Not until she was nearly there did it dawn on her that Toby might also be present, and she would probably meet him. The thought didn't trouble her. How far away he seemed now!

They found most of the family in the supper room, where Maria and Sarah were tucking in with a vengeance. Maria was dressed like a young girl in a low-cut gown of ivory silk. Her head sported a jeweled turban, extravagantly adorned with ostrich feathers that shook as she ate. Sarah, too, wore clothes that were several decades too young for her, topped off with a new wig of gleaming gold curls. They greeted Calvina with screams of delight, and she responded politely.

Eglantine bounced in with two young men in tow. Her dress looked as if it had been pulled about, and she was tipsy. "I never had so much fun in my life." she squealed. "Why, Calvina! Fancy seeing you!"

181

Calvina suddenly became aware that she must still look a little disheveled and hastened to straighten her attire. Eglantine tittered. "I declare, you've been enjoying yourself with your lovers!"

"No such thing," Calvina said calmly. "One gentleman made a cake of himself, but I dealt with him. He'll be more cautious next time."

"What happened to your domino?" Maria demanded of her husband, inspecting the ruined garment.

"I was obliged to rescue Calvina from attack," Hugh said quickly. A cynical snort from his wife made him add, "Isn't that so, Calvina?"

Calvina gave him a look of scorn and turned away without answering. Through the open door of the supper room she could see Toby sitting at cards. There was a terrible, motionless intensity about him that made Calvina's heart sink. The whole Dalrymple family had battened on him. Whatever the size of his fortune, it hadn't been enough to sustain the burden. Now he was gambling because he desperately needed money.

As she watched, the game ended, and Toby's sagging shoulders told their own story. He saw her and a look of despair settled over his face as he approached her. "Now you know how I live," he said with a wan smile.

"For pity's sake, leave London!" she urged him. "This life is ruinous."

"I know it." He sighed.

"Then you simply must do something. Don't let the Dalrymples live off you."

His only response was a helpless shrug. Calvina stared at him, aghast. He could do nothing, she realized. What she'd thought was generous forbearance was no more than weakness. She pitied him with all her heart, but she also wondered how she could ever have thought herself in love with him.

"Aylesbury," came a voice from within the card room. "We're starting another game. Are you in?"

"No," Calvina said urgently.

"You don't understand," he pleaded. "I'm in debt."

"And you'll get in deeper if you don't stop now."

"Come on, Aylesbury," someone called. "It's a chance to recoup your losses."

He looked at her helplessly before returning to the card room. Calvina watched him as he sat down at the table, his head bent, as if to a yoke. After a moment, she turned away, knowing that she had said a final good-bye to Toby.

The Haddens had turned into a merry family party, with two betrothals to celebrate. Calvina joined them to drink their healths in champagne and was heartily toasted in return for her part in bringing each couple together.

Mr. Simmington reappeared and swept her off to see the Covington ruin. It stood on a slight incline, bathed in moonlight, its gargoyles seeming to scream out overhead. Calvina shivered pleasurably. It looked just as a ruin should, with moss in all the right places, gothic arches, and a multitude of shadows.

"You'll think me a shocking provincial dowdy," she said, laughing, "but I love to think of all the dramatic things that must have happened here before it fell into disrepair. Look at that darkened doorway. Surely a shrouded figure will appear any moment and moan at us."

Mr. Simmington looked at her quizzically. "But, my dear lady, surely you realize—?"

He got no further. A grinding noise overhead made him look up sharply and gasp. Calvina followed his gaze and saw, with horror, that a heavy gargoyle had detached itself and was hurtling toward her. Her limbs seemed petrified with shock, but somehow she forced them to react and moved just in time to flatten herself against the wall. The next minute something hit her on the head and she fell to the ground.

She came around to find herself lying on a bed, with Lady Covington hovering anxiously at the foot. A strong pair of arms was holding her but at first she was too dazed to think about this.

"Thank God!" Lady Covington said. "The doctor will be here directly."

She bustled out and now Calvina became aware of the other person in the room, holding her. It was Rupert.

"Be still," he told her gently. "You are lucky to be alive."

"What—what happened?"

"A gargoyle fell. Thank God it missed you, but a chip flew off and struck your head."

"How do you come to be here?" she whispered.

"Never mind that now. Don't worry about anything. If the doctor says you can be moved I'll take you home directly."

"It's nothing," Calvina said huskily. "I shall be well, by and by. Take me home, Rupert."

"We'll wait for the doctor." He laid her back against the pillows.

"You won't go, will you?" She clung to him.

"No, I'll stay with you." He poured her a glass of wine and was administering it when the doctor was announced. He pronounced her wound little more than a graze.

"I think you collapsed more from shock than from injury," he declared. "A good rest will restore you."

Lady Covington would have had her stay for the night, but Calvina was eager to return home with Rupert and be alone with him. In the carriage he held her close while they traveled the short distance to Berkeley Square.

"How did you come to be there?" she asked hazily.

"I returned early from Bath and followed you." He discouraged further speech by pressing her head against his shoulder. Calvina thought she felt his lips brush her forehead.

When she was settled in bed Rupert held something to her lips. "Drink this," he ordered quietly.

"But this—isn't laudanum . . ." she said. "The doctor . . ."

"Doctors don't always know best. This is something of my own, that will be better for you. Trust me . . . trust me . . ."

She could still hear the echoing of his voice as she fell asleep. She slept for most of the following day. Her dreams were filled with disturbing memories of the masquerade. Simmington had seen Rupert arrive, he'd hinted as much. But that had been early in the evening.

"Why did you take so long to find me?" she whispered.

"I couldn't discover you in that crush. Hush now, don't talk. Don't think of it. Forget everything that happened—forget—forget—"

The darkness enveloped her again, and when she awoke the next day she felt well and strong. There was none of the drugged feeling that laudanum could leave behind, and she realized that Rupert's draft really had done her good.

She tried to think back over the masquerade, and found, to her surprise, that she could remember very little. She knew a gargoyle had fallen, but when she tried to recall details the incident seemed to have retreated to the back of her mind.

To her delight, Rupert had brought Ninian to town, and he joined her downstairs. "Thank God you're safe!" he said fervently. "When I heard what had happened, I feared such things . . ."

"It was only an accident," Calvina said, smiling.

"An accident. Yes, of course. How could it have been anything else?" His voice had a feverish note that puzzled her.

"The gargoyle came loose," she said, frowning as she tried to think. "I'm sure it was that—in the ruins—they're so old—"

"But they're not," Ninian said in a strained tone. "That 'ruin' is no more than a folly." When she looked puzzled he said, "A few years back there was a craze for ruins.

185

They were supposed to be romantic. People who didn't have them had them erected specially."

"You mean people actually *built* ruins?" Calvina demanded, astonished.

"People with more money then sense, yes. The Covingtons built theirs about five years ago."

"So that's why everything looked so perfect," she said, dazed. "It was *too* perfect."

"I'm sure every foolish fantasy was catered for," Ninian replied dryly. "The point is that it's practically a new building. It should have been safe. Calvina, are you certain that you and Simmington were the only ones there?"

"I'm not sure of anything." She frowned. "It's all become so vague."

"Perhaps when the laudanum wears off . . ."

"I didn't have any. Rupert gave me a draft of his own."

A terrible stillness seemed to settle over Ninian. "Rupert gave you something he'd made up himself?"

"Yes. I have it here. He left some by me because I find it excellent." He took the little blue bottle from her and studied it closely. Something about it seemed to fascinate him. "Why are you staring at it like that?" she asked.

"Nothing—no reason. I just wish that your memory was clearer." He replaced the bottle on the table beside her. "Would you know if there'd been someone behind the wall?"

"You mean, someone who might have shouted a warning?"

He hesitated a moment before saying awkwardly, "Yes, that is what I meant, of course."

"Did you see nobody yourself?"

"I wasn't there. Rupert invited me to accompany him, but I preferred to retire early. I wish now that I'd been there to watch over you."

"Now, how could I need that, when I have Rupert to watch over me?" she asked gaily.

186

"Yes, of course. It's just that—my God! what am I saying? If you'll excuse me, I have pressing letters to write."

He began to leave the room, but at the door he halted and turned back to her, almost as though against his will. "Calvina, that time at Glennister Court, when you were nearly shot—was Rupert with you?"

"Yes, we'd ridden out together."

"Thank God!" he said in relief.

"But you know he was with me," she said, puzzled. "You saw us return together."

"But I meant—was he actually with you when the shot was fired?"

"No, he'd ridden off to surprise some poachers."

"But you could still see him?"

"No. Ninian, I don't understand. What are you saying?"

"Nothing. Nothing at all. I must be mad to imagine for a moment—please, forget that I spoke."

"But how can I when you say such strange things? What does it matter where Rupert was?"

"It doesn't, of course," he said hastily. "I told you I was mad. It's only that I'd feel easier in my mind if they'd caught the man who fired."

Suddenly his real meaning burst upon her. "Ninian!" she exclaimed, aghast. "You can't mean that you suspect my husband of trying to—oh, I can't even say the words! It's insane! Impossible!"

"Yes, impossible," he echoed eagerly. "How could I have such thoughts about a man who is my dearest friend, as well as my kin? It's only the unlucky accident of his being there and out of sight when these things happened. Calvina, I beg you to say nothing of this to Rupert. I couldn't look him in the face again."

"I certainly won't tell him," she said indignantly. "I don't know what maggot has got into your head, Ninian, but I know this isn't really you talking."

"Forgive me. It's just that the news I heard this morning has disturbed me, perhaps more than it should."

"What news? What has happened to disturb you?"

"Ah, so you haven't heard! Lord Ullaston died last night."

Chapter Eleven

Within hours all London knew the uplifting story of how Lord Ullaston's final moments had been spent in the bosom of his family, sons and daughters gathered around his bed, weeping as they listened to his edifying last words.

"Not if I know that family," Rupert observed grimly. "I'll wager a monkey James had a lawyer in tow."

"Two lawyers, actually," Mr. Simmington said with malicious satisfaction. "The doctor says the howling and wailing carried the old boy off several hours ahead of time. And they weren't all by the bed, whatever you may have heard. The daughters stripped Lysandra's room. She'd taken her jewelry out of the bank, to keep it safe she thought. They took every last trinket. She's penniless."

"Ullaston left her a handsome jointure," Rupert said, frowning.

"James is bent on oversetting it. He claims to have gotten his father's signature on a piece of paper that entitles him to every penny, and locked Lysandra in her room."

"Then I think it's time an old friend paid her a visit of condolence," Rupert said grimly.

He was gone for over an hour. Calvina, returning during that time, found the servants in a bustle.

"It wasn't my fault, my lady," the porter insisted tearfully. "She just marched in past me. And me not knowing what to do . . ."

"It's all right, Albert," Calvina reassured him gently. "Just tell me who is here."

"Lady Ullaston, my lady. She arrived in a hack not half an hour ago, and you and the master being out . . ."

"Never mind. Where is she?"

"In the library, my lady."

Calvina knew only that Lord Ullaston was dead. Owing to the time she spent at Trident House the more lurid of the other stories had passed her by. She hardly knew what to expect as she slipped quietly into the library, and was taken aback by the sight of the figure stretched out on the window seat in an attitude of complete abandon.

Every stitch of Lady Ullaston's clothing was black, from the voluminous silk pelisse trimmed with sable, to the huge veil that covered her elegant hat and swept almost to the ground front and back. She was apparently convulsed by heartrending sobs, but something about them caused Calvina's ready compassion to drain away. They had a theatrical sound, and she could have sworn they'd started only when the door opened.

At the sound of her feet on the polished floor Lysandra raised her head a little, her hands still covering her face outside her veil, and uttered a shriek.

"Ah, I thank God you have come, you have come! My dearest friend, my only friend. If you knew how they have treated me, spurned by all."

Calvina stood as though turned to stone. Her eyes were wide with horror as she looked down at the figure, writhing with some emotion that might have been grief.

The imploring voice rose to a wail. "You swore that no one should come between us. What will I do if you spurn me now? See, I cast myself on my knees before you, a woman who ruined herself gladly for love of you. You promised that you would protect and love me forever."

There was a click as the library door opened. Rupert stood on the threshold, taking in the scene before him: Calvina, transfixed by horror, Lysandra kneeling in an abandon of woe. He uttered a soft curse and strode across to seize Lysandra by the elbows and draw her to her feet.

"There's no need for this," he said curtly. He resisted her attempts to cast herself on his breast and sat her back firmly on the window seat.

"Rupert," Calvina said in a low voice. "What is this woman doing here?"

He replied to Lysandra. "I called on you, but they said you'd left the house."

"It is false!" Lysandra shrieked. "They locked me up. James has forged his father's signature on a paper denying me my rightful inheritance. He's trying to get me to sign something saying I've stolen from the family. I escaped and came here—homeless, penniless . . ."

"Then naturally I must help you. James can't be allowed to get away with this." He lifted the long veil so that her face was revealed, distraught and streaming with tears that in no way marred her beauty. Calvina's nails dug into her hands. She longed to tear this flaunting creature from her husband and hurl her out into the street, where she belonged. But long training in charity restrained her. Nor would her pride let her reveal her feelings to her husband.

"I'm a poor, homeless widow," Lysandra whispered. "What help can there be for me?"

"Don't make it worse by indulging in melodramatics," Rupert told her, kindly but firmly. "Both my wife and I are your friends, and will stand by you." His eyes met Calvina's, and she read in them a command that she confirm his words. She stood silent, unable to speak, almost unable to breathe.

"My wife joins me in an invitation to remain with us until your affairs are settled," he said in a harsh voice. *"Is that not so, Calvina?"*

"Of course," she forced herself to say tonelessly. "I will order the housekeeper to prepare a room."

She almost stumbled out of the library, her mind whirling in anguish. How could Rupert ask her to receive his mistress, to welcome this shameless woman as if they had never been lovers? If he had so little regard for the decencies, what else was he planning? A divorce, so that he could marry Lysandra? He would become an outcast from society again, but did he care anymore? He'd tasted respectability, and now, perhaps, was bored with it, as, sooner or later, he grew bored with everything.

She performed her duties mechanically, instructing the housekeeper, and informing the butler that there would be one more for dinner. Somehow she did these things with a cheerful face so that the servants wouldn't know the horror inside her. She even forced herself to show her unwanted guest to her room, and offer her an arm in support, since Lysandra was still, apparently, in a state of collapse.

When that duty was over she ran back to the library, where Rupert still was. "How dare you ask me to entertain that woman!" she demanded stormily.

"I had no choice," he said curtly. "The Ullastons have thrown her out."

"And so you of all people must take her in? You dare to ask me to receive your mistress!"

He stared at her strangely. "If she were my mistress I would not ask you to receive her. I don't deny our past relationship, but that's long over."

"I do not—" She stopped as she saw where her fury was leading her. She'd been on the verge of calling him a liar, but she had no proof. All she knew for certain was that the mere sight of Lysandra Ullaston roused a storm of jealous misery in her breast.

"You do not what?" he demanded, looking at her closely. "I hope you weren't going to say that you don't believe me."

"How do I know what to believe? You don't deny your relations with her—"

"Which I have told you are in the past. I'm trying now to avoid a scandal."

"By bringing her here?" she demanded scornfully.

"If it's true that she has no money and no place to sleep—and I believe it is—then she's safer here than outside, spreading wild stories to the world. She comes to *us*, both of us, because we are her friends."

"She's no friend of mine."

"Then you're very foolish. Act the part of her friend, receive her with complaisance, and there will be no scandal. Throw her out, and tongues will never stop wagging."

She knew that he was right, but she was too angry to think rationally. "And I tell you that I will not be complaisant. I've given her a room, as you wished, but I refuse to be in this house while she is here."

"Thus really giving the gossips something to talk about," he snapped.

"Let them say what they like. Is it any more than the truth?"

"Beware, Calvina—"

"Oh yes, you'd like to silence me, wouldn't you? You'd like me to give you my countenance while you and she live together in this house—"

"I've told you it's only until her affairs are sorted out."

"And how long will that take? Months? Years?"

He stared at her. "I've never seen you like this before—"

"Because my eyes were never opened before. Either you tell that woman to leave tomorrow, or I'll tell her myself."

His face grew hard. "I don't like ultimatums."

"It's her or me, Rupert. Get rid of her, or I leave."

She turned to go, but he grasped her arm and forced her around to face him. "I have told you what you will do. You will obey me and remain here."

"I won't . . ." she whispered. She felt as though she were suffocating.

"You'll do as I say. I am dealing with this situation in my own way, and I will not have you interfere. Do you

193

understand?" When she didn't answer, his gaze intensified. "Answer me, Calvina. Do you understand?"

"Yes," she said hoarsely. She was transfixed by the look in his eyes, terrified of it.

"Good. As long as we understand each other, there's no need for this fuss." As he spoke he was drawing her nearer, until her head was against his shoulder and his lips brushed hers. "Trust me, my wife," he murmured. "You've trusted me before. Trust me now."

She wanted to struggle free of his grasp, but her limbs felt as though weighed down by lead. Despite her anger and fear of him she found that he could cast the dark spell as easily as ever. The warmth of passion crept through her body, defying her attempts to resist it. The touch of his lips was as devastating as ever. She knew this was no gesture of love, but an assertion of control. He was telling her that she could never defy him because he owned her body and soul. And she was powerless to refuse.

"Tell me that you trust me," he whispered against her lips.

She tried to say the words, but they wouldn't come. After a moment she felt him grow tense and cold. One look into her face told him the truth. His face was terrible as he set her aside and left the room.

Calvina waited for a long moment before following him. She needed time to calm the turbulence in her breast. In the past she had sparred with him, been angry with him, laughed with him, and loved him passionately. Now, for the first time, she felt that she could hate him, and the feeling appalled her.

Hurrying up to the wing of the house where her own and Rupert's apartments lay, she found Lysandra in a corridor close by. "Your bedroom is in another part of the house," she said coldly.

"Oh yes," Lysandra said quickly. "I came here seeking you, Lady Rupert. But you weren't in your room."

"Indeed? And in what way may I serve you?"

194

"I—I had something to say to you—but I forget now what it was."

A child wouldn't have been deceived by such a story, Calvina thought bitterly. This woman had come openly to Rupert's room and sought to cover it with an unconvincing tale. Why did they bother, since they clearly thought she could be forced into submission? They would learn that they were wrong.

"Let me escort you back to your own room." She took Lysandra's arm firmly. "I suggest you rest there until dinner, which will be in an hour."

Only her training in fortitude got her through that ghastly dinner. Rupert spoke gently to Lysandra, as though trying to rally her from a grief that he knew better than anyone she didn't really feel. Sometimes he would draw Calvina into the conversation, as though he were not yet lost to the proprieties. She would respond with smiles that amazed her.

The three of them retired early. Calvina sat tensely in her bedroom, wondering if he would be so shameless as to go to that woman tonight.

But it was to her that he came. He was frowning, but he spoke mildly. "You did well tonight," he said. "Come, let us not quarrel. I will forget what you said this afternoon, since I cannot believe that you meant it." As he spoke he reached out to her, but instinctively she backed away from him.

"No, Rupert."

"Are you refusing me?"

"I've done all you asked. Let that be enough. I'm tired tonight, and have the headache."

"In that case, I won't trouble you," he said lightly. "Good night, dear wife."

Now he would go to Lysandra, she thought angrily. Perhaps she should have let him stay, made love to him. But her soul revolted at the thought of going through the motions of passion, knowing that his true desire was for another woman. She had loved him. In

195

some desolate corner of her heart she loved him still. She would flee and never see him again rather than accept second best.

It was true that she had the headache. The evening had been a torture to her. If only she could sleep, then perhaps she could think clearly.

From a small cabinet near her bed she took the little blue bottle containing the draft Rupert had made up for her. Too tired to think clearly, she put it to her lips and sipped some of the liquid before she recollected whence it came. Then she set it down sharply.

"I must be losing my mind," she murmured to herself. "I've let Ninian's suspicions affect me, although I know them to be madness."

But that had been before Rupert had forced her to entertain his mistress who was now free to marry him. Bathed in love for her husband, convinced that his feelings for her were deeper than he could express, it had been easy—or at least possible—then to laugh such suspicions aside. But now . . .

She stared at the bottle, trying to pick it up and drink again. But she couldn't force herself to do it, and at last she got into bed.

Despite her anguish she soon fell into a doze, but found no peace in it. She seemed caught between sleep and wakefulness, unable to be wholly conscious or unconscious. Terrible images danced through her head. She fled them but they were behind and before, mocking as they pursued her, then turning to menace her. Her body was racked with pain. She dreamed that she rose from her bed and retched violently, then staggered back, weakened almost to death.

Rupert appeared hovering over her, and she whispered in horror, "You have poisoned me."

"Of course, my dear. You are of no further use to me. Now you must die." He seemed to speak without moving his lips, while the fires of hell burned brightly behind him.

By their light she relived the moments that had terrified her since their marriage: the runaway hack that could have made her miscarry, if, as he'd believed, she'd been carrying Toby's child; the shots from "poachers" who were never caught; the stone that had been mysteriously dislodged from a new building. He'd been there at the masquerade, unknown to her. Simmington had seen him arrive much earlier, had wondered at their not being together. But Rupert had kept out of sight, awaiting his moment.

And finally the poison, from a draft that he had made up. Why had she taken the risk of drinking from that bottle? But she knew the answer. It was because even then hope had lingered. No more hope now.

Lysandra was there with him, in his arms, smiling up into his face. Together they laughed at the woman who had loved him, innocently and with all her heart. They were two of a kind, and they knew that only fools trust the devil. She had been a fool and was paying for it now, with the knowledge that the man she loved was trying to kill her.

At last the dreams ceased, and she lay motionless, locked in a cold place where there was only despair. When she opened her eyes the early dawn had turned her room to gray, as gray as her heart.

She understood Ninian's warning now. Rupert had soon regretted his marriage and had arranged a series of "accidents" to dispose of her so that he could marry Lysandra. She'd deluded herself into thinking that he loved her, and now her heart was breaking with the truth.

She rose and found herself trembling but able to stand. She'd taken enough poison to make her ill but stopped before she drank a lethal dose. Her one thought now was to escape. If she could reach Bath Ninian would protect her.

In her weakened state it took a while to dress herself, but at last she managed it. One small bag contained all she would need for the journey. She would travel by the mail coach.

She crept down the stairs as quietly as she could, stopping now and then to hold her breath, because already the underservants were rising. They would get the kitchen range going, make tea, and take it to the housekeeper and butler. The way to the side door led past the kitchen, but luckily the door was almost closed, and she was able to slip by unobserved.

She found a hack quickly and was soon at the General Post Office, from where the mail departed. To her relief there was one leaving in a few minutes. She hurried and took her seat with the other three passengers. The mails were almost twice as fast as the coaches, because they were more lightly built, accepted only four passengers, and took precedence over everything else on the road. Since they also changed horses every eight miles and could travel at the incredible speed of nine miles an hour she knew she could be in Bath by evening.

As the mail moved off out of the yard she gave a sigh of relief at seeing that there was no one in pursuit of her. Now she could sit back and try to rest her aching head. It was a relief, but only for a while. There were many miles and many hours to go before she could yield to her grief.

The light was fading when a hired coach pulled up at Belmont. To her relief, Ninian was there. She ran into his study and found him pouring over some papers at the desk. He glanced up as the door was flung open, and one look at her face told him everything. He opened his arms and the next moment she was in them.

He didn't say anything at first, just held her for a long moment while she sobbed her heart out.

"You fill me with fear," he said at last. "Tell me what has happened."

"Ullaston is dead"—she choked—"and Rupert has taken Lysandra into the house—forced me to accept her—and last night he tried to poison me."

198

"My God," he breathed. "I've always known that he could be a bad man, but not this bad. Force you to accept his mistress in your home—not even Rupert could do such a thing—surely—?"

"He denied she's his mistress," she cried wildly, "said their affair was in the past—"

"But it isn't," Ninian said harshly. "I may be out of the way here, but I have friends who write to me. It's the talk of society how he flaunts her even while he pretends to be a good husband to you. Thank God you saw the truth in time and came to me."

"You're the only friend I can trust, Ninian."

"And Aunt Josie. She doesn't know the truth about him, and I'm afraid she'll be hurt when we tell her. But she'll stand firm for you. The sooner I can get you to Glennister Court the better."

"But—can't you keep me here?" she asked wildly.

"Not without ruining your reputation. My dear, I'm a single man. You can't pass the night under my roof."

"But you're my husband's cousin—"

"A husband you've fled because he tried to take your life. That's bound to come out, and people will wonder why you came here. I'm afraid they'll reach scandalous conclusions, and I wouldn't harm you for the world.

"I'll have food and wine sent to you, and when you're rested you must seek the protection of Aunt Josie's chaperonage. Just for tonight. Tomorrow I'll get you right away. Don't be afraid. Rupert can't reach here before tomorrow."

She yielded to his persuasions. The refreshments that were served reminded her that she hadn't eaten for nearly twenty-four hours. They couldn't ease her misery, but they restored her strength and made her feel able to face her trials.

At last Ninian took her out to the carriage. Halton, his devoted groom, was sitting on the box, and she thought he gave her a strange look. But then, all the world looked strange to her now.

"Suppose Aunt Josie thinks I'm mad," she fretted as they started their journey. "How can I tell her such things?"

"No need. I've sent a groom over there with a letter breaking it to her. Josie isn't blind to Rupert. She once hinted to me that he has depths of evil that only she knows of. She loves him in spite of everything, but she won't side with him in this wickedness."

In a short time they were drawing up outside the great house, and Josie was advancing down the steps to welcome her. She couldn't help remembering her other arrival here, on the night of her wedding. Then, too, Josie had embraced her without question. Calvina had to fight back the tears at the memory.

"Come inside," Josie said, clasping her warmly. "And you're not to say a word until you've rested thoroughly."

It was bliss to give herself into Josie's kindly hands, to be led to the fire, and to drink the wine that appeared on a table beside her.

"Ninian told me everything in his letter," Josie said, facing her with compassion in her wise, tired eyes.

"I know you'll find it hard to believe—" Calvina began.

"Alas, my dear, I'm afraid I don't. I've known Rupert all his life and—well, let's just say that I believe you. It's sad and terrible." She sighed.

"I've promised to get Calvina away tomorrow," Ninian said. "Whatever happens, Rupert mustn't force his presence on her again."

"Of course, my dear boy. You did quite right to bring her to me. But do go home now, and let poor Calvina get some sleep."

Ninian took Calvina's hand, pressed his lips against it reverently, and left the room.

"If only I could think straight," Calvina said huskily.

"Best if you don't try to think at all," Josie said, looking at her strangely. "There'll be time to think later. Now you must sleep."

200

"Yes, I can hardly keep my eyes open." She shook her head, which seemed to be unusually heavy. "You tried to warn me, the day we married, didn't you? You said, 'Whatever made you do it?' You knew what he was like."

"But it was too late then," Josie pointed out. "You were already married."

"Yes, it was too late," Calvina said sadly.

Something about the room seemed odd. The curtains had been pulled, but the ones shielding the French doors had a gap, through which she could see that the doors themselves were still open. It was dark outside, and a wind was getting up that made the curtain billow.

"I'm cold," she whispered.

"You'll feel that way, at first," Josie said, not taking her eyes off her. "And then you'll sleep peacefully. Try to be calm and believe that all will be well."

"But—all is not well," Calvina said wildly. She struggled to her feet, overwhelmed by terror as the truth became horribly clear. "You deceived me."

"Only because I had to," Josie said. "Rupert thought it best if we did it this way."

"Rupert thought—you're in league with him," she gasped. "You're a part of this—"

"Let's just say that I'm following his wishes. I would never go against him, you know."

Calvina summoned all her strength to scream. "Ninian—*Ninian!*"

"Ninian's gone," Josie said. "Don't waste your breath calling for him."

"The wine was drugged—you tricked me—oh God!"

The curtains billowed and the candles flickered in the wind. Calvina fought to clear her head, but everything seemed to have lost its outline. She blinked hard, and when she looked again, Rupert was standing before her.

"You can't be here," she gasped. "You're an illusion— if I touch you, you'll disappear."

She staggered toward the figure, her hand outstretched. At the last moment she swayed. Rupert caught her, drawing her against him and looking down into her face. Hazily, she looked up and saw the face of Satan looming over her.

"I'm sorry, my dear," he said. "I hadn't meant it to come to this, but you were getting too suspicious. Now I must end everything quickly."

She fainted as he raised her in his arms.

Chapter Twelve

Later that night a carriage drew up outside Lord Rupert's house in Bath. Sam, the steward, appeared at once, like a man who'd been watching. He hurriedly opened the door of the carriage and Lord Rupert stepped out, carrying a figure swathed in a large cloak, its face hidden. Aunt Josie followed him into the house, and Sam quickly closed the door behind her.

Most of the servants had been given the night off and ordered to keep well clear of the house. Only a few were about, and of these only Sam was allowed to witness the arrival. He knew who it was who lay insensible in his master's arms and knew also what would happen next. He averted his eyes from that helpless figure. He was nervous of what was required of him this night, but he would obey Rupert without question.

Without a word Rupert carried Calvina up the stairs to a small room at the very top of the house. It was little more than an attic, furnished with a spartan bed, a chair, and a low table. A huge window occupied most of one wall.

He laid her on the bed and held her for a moment, her head thrown back against his shoulder. In just this way had he cradled her in their nights of passion. She'd looked up at him, not silent and still as she was now, but with her face wild with love and joy. The memory smote him, and for the first time he doubted if he could carry this deed through to the end.

"I suppose I'm doing the right thing?" he said slowly.

"What choice was there?" his aunt asked. "There's nothing to do with a mistake but put it right. You said so yourself."

"Yes, but this way . . ." His wife's pale face seemed to reproach him.

"It's too late to fret now," she said. "Things must take their course. You'll be glad afterward."

"Afterward," he echoed. "Things will seem so strange— afterward." He laid Calvina back against the pillows. "When I've gone, lock the door," he said curtly, and departed.

Sam was waiting outside. "Allow nobody near this door," Rupert commanded him. "Nobody at all."

The room came into focus gradually. Calvina had opened her eyes only slightly, so that for a moment she could see without being noticed. She didn't recognize the room, and this all seemed of a piece with the monstrous nightmare in which she was living.

She could see Aunt Josie, sitting by the bed, watching her carefully. She remembered now that, under cover of helping her, Josie had drugged her, to deliver her into Rupert's hands. Her gorge rose to think that sweet, elderly face should hide such wickedness and deceit.

She was about to speak, but, as though a warning hand had fallen on her shoulder, she felt something stop her. She'd taken in the fact that she and Josie were alone. The door was bound to be locked, and there might be someone outside, but fate had presented her with one chance, if only she could take it. . . .

She opened her eyes wide, and smiled at Josie. "Hallo, Aunt," she said sleepily. "How comforting to find you with me."

Josie leaned forward. "Do you know where you are, my dear?" she said gently.

"Why, I'm at Glennister Court. You said I'd be safe with you, and I'm sure I will be."

Josie patted her hand. "You're going to be quite safe, my dear. There's nothing to worry about anymore."

"I'm terribly thirsty."

"I'll pour you some wine." Josie rose and walked to a low table.

"No, not wine," Calvina said at once. "I want fresh water. Please, do get me some."

"I'll fetch it from downstairs. Rest until I come back."

Josie left the room, locking the door behind her. As soon as she'd gone Calvina rose from the bed. She had to steady herself, for the effects of the drug were still on her, but she forced herself to be strong.

Apart from the locked door the only exit was the window. Calvina pushed it open and looked out, but realized with dismay that she was high up at the top of the house. It was hard to discern much from this height, but the shape of the roofs seemed familiar, and she guessed she was in Rupert's Bath lodgings.

It was clear now why he hadn't bothered to lock the window as well. Far below her was the area leading to the basement, surrounded by iron railings topped by lethal spikes. There were more railings on the steps that led down into the area. Even if it were possible to jump from this height, she would only end up impaled on the spikes.

She heard footsteps outside and flattened herself against the wall, looking for a weapon. Then a soft voice said, "Calvina?"

"Ninian!" she cried with relief. "Oh, thank God! Ninian I'm here. Let me out."

There was the reassuring sound of the key in the lock, and the next moment Ninian stood in the doorway. Frantic with relief he threw herself into his arms. "Oh, Ninian, I'm so glad you came. We must get away quickly. Rupert brought me here to kill me. . . ."

Her voice faded at what she saw. A familiar figure lay crumpled on the stairs, in an attitude of unconsciousness.

"Aunt Josie!" she gasped.

"It was the only way I could get the key," Ninian said.

And Josie was her enemy, Calvina reminded herself. Yet there was something about such ruthlessness that made her uneasy. Slowly she looked up and her blood ran cold as she read the truth in Ninian's face, but before she could speak he'd thrust her violently back into the room and turned the key, locking the two of them in.

"I'm sorry, Calvina, but this has gone as far as I dare let it."

"Ninian—I don't understand—"

But she did. It was there in Ninian's eyes, so much colder than she'd ever realized.

"You!" she cried. "It was you, all the time."

"Of course," he said in the quiet voice she knew, but which suddenly sounded terrifying. "I'm surprised you never guessed before. I've always admired your sharp intelligence. If only you hadn't married Rupert, what a wife you would have made for me! But you did marry him, and I'm afraid that rash act was your death warrant."

"But why?" she asked, playing for time.

"Don't worry, I'm not going to kill you just yet, maybe not for half an hour. It depends on how long it takes Rupert to get here."

"Rupert—?"

"Halton kept watch and told me he'd brought you here. Then he went to Belmont, looking for me. I've left a message to say where I am, and Rupert will follow me.

"He has to die before I can inherit. I thought he would never marry, you know. I was content to be his heir, and if he found a bride at last—well, she could have had an accident before the wedding. But he sprung you on me without warning, and I had to find another way, before you had a son.

"I thought of killing him at once, but it was too uncertain. You might already be carrying his child. At one

206

time I thought you *were*. I had to do something quickly, just in case."

"The hack that ran away with me," she said with dawning comprehension. "That was *you*?"

"No, Halton. He'll do anything I ask. I sent him to London to watch you. He knew all about your night visits, and the hack that was already waiting for you. He presented himself one night, and you got in, as he'd hoped."

"I was suppose to miscarry, wasn't I?" she asked bitterly.

"I hadn't bargained for your having the nerve to jump out. But it didn't matter. I soon realized you weren't pregnant. It gave me more time to work in secret. That's always been my strength, you see, that nobody suspected me."

"Oh my God!" she breathed. "All this time I've liked you, trusted you—"

"Of course. That was essential. Ninian, the poor relation who can be relied on to efface himself, like a dummy, with no heart." Suddenly his face changed, became distorted with passion. "But I have a heart. I can love. I loved Lord Thomas better than Rupert ever did, because I'm like him. Underneath. Where nobody sees. I love the estate, and I knew long ago that it *had* to be mine.

"Rupert played into my hands. 'Devil Glennister,' who'd commit any act of wickedness, including murdering his wife. And when they hanged him, everything would be mine.

"You made it a little difficult by fleeing London. I could only act when the two of you were together, and he would look guilty. But luckily Rupert followed you down here. I guessed he would, and that he'd go to Glennister Court first. That's why I insisted on taking you there.

"He's been getting suspicious of me, and this may be

my last chance, so I've got to succeed now. How obliging of you to make your suspicion of him so plain."

"All those accidents," Calvina said in a dazed voice. "How could you do it?"

"Very easily. The day you were nearly shot by 'poachers,' I was returning to Belmont in the dawn when I saw you and Rupert. I always carried a gun. I fired in the copse, then moved closer to you while he went to investigate. Everyone knew you'd gone out alone together. Unfortunately I couldn't get close enough, and missed you. If I'd hit you I'd have thrown the gun away—one of Rupert's by the way—and let it be found.

"I returned to Belmont, and no one knew I'd ever been near you. The gargoyle was easier. When Rupert had followed you to the masquerade, I 'retired to my room,' then slipped out without any of the servants seeing me. In a domino it was simple to mingle with the crowd, awaiting my chance. I had to do everything on the spur of the moment and use whatever came to hand. That was why I failed so often. I couldn't organize properly, you see.

"But no matter. I was able to plant the seed of suspicion in your mind the next day. You refused to believe me, but I think a little doubt remained. I daresay people will have noticed that doubt, and remember it when you're dead."

The casual mention of her death sent a cold tremor through her, but Calvina refused to yield to her fear. It was important to keep Ninian talking as long as possible.

"But the poison," she managed to say. "You weren't there. That couldn't have been Halton."

"No, Lady Ullaston. She'd already helped me once, by sending for the Aylesburys—"

"*You* told her about them?"

"Of course. I've been in contact with her all the time. At the start, you see, I was still toying with the idea of

Rupert divorcing you. Then I could have killed him outright later, and married you myself. So much more reliable than this indirect way. But that plan misfired. Instead of casting you off he swept you out of the ballroom, so I've heard. When I next saw the two of you, you were smelling of April and May. A considerable setback for me.

"I made use of Lysandra one last time. I'm as at home in Rupert's laboratory as he is; more in fact, because Lord Thomas taught me his own skills with poisons. I made some up, put it in one of Rupert's blue medicine bottles, and gave it to Lysandra. She slipped into your room yesterday and left it in exchange for the one you already had. She thought if you were dead Rupert would marry her. She's too stupid to see that he might be blamed. I'm surprised the poison didn't kill you, but I suppose you didn't drink enough. So I'll have to do the job myself.

"How fortunate that Rupert sent most of his servants away tonight. There'll be only Sam to deal with, and Halton will back my story. Rupert brought you here to kill you. I followed, hoping to prevent a murder. Alas, too late! He clubbed you to death and threw your body from that window, meaning to tell the world that you fell. Josie was his accomplice so he killed her, too, to ensure her silence.

"Both bodies will be found on the railings, and the world will know that your last words were an accusation of your husband."

"No," she whispered, backing away from him. *"No—"*

"But, Calvina, I have no choice. Surely you can see that? Please don't think I like doing this. I told you once I loved you. It was true. If you'd responded to me just a little I'd simply have killed Rupert, and we could have been married after his death. But you never cared for me."

She'd retreated as far as the wall. Ninian followed her

and stood close, speaking softly. She could see his eyes—cold, mad eyes. How long ago had he gone mad, brooding over the thing he loved and was determined to have?

"What a wife you would have made for me!"

"Never," Calvina said fiercely. "I could never have loved you."

His mouth twisted cruelly. "The more fool you! The sooner this is over the better. I think I hear him arriving, and it'll be more convenient if you're dead before he gets here."

He seized her roughly by the shoulders. Calvina fought fiercely but she was still weak from the drug and she knew she had no chance. Inexorably he drew her to the bed, tossed her down, and seized the pillow. As she saw it descend on her face she knew, with horror, that she was going to die, and the man she loved would be blamed. All her failing strength went into her final, despairing scream.

"Calvina!"

Was she mad or dreaming? The voice was Rupert's. It was followed by a thundering on the door. Ninian cursed and pressed the pillow hard, but she managed to turn her head aside, giving herself a few more precious moments of air. She used them to cry out Rupert's name. The sound seemed to redouble his resolve, for the next moment the door flew open and almost off its hinges. Rupert was across the room in two steps, his face murderous as he pulled Ninian away from her, and slammed him against the wall.

Ninian made no effort to fight back, but stayed, heaving violently and clutching the wall for support. Most of the breath had been knocked out of his body.

Rupert drew Calvina from the bed and held her tightly, although his eyes never left his cousin. "Are you all right?" he demanded.

"Yes," she said breathlessly. "You came just in time."

"And it's as well for you that I did," Rupert said to Ninian. "My God, I only half believed it! When I first began to suspect you I told myself not to indulge foolish fancies. *You*, the one man I believed truly my friend! A man to whom I've given every sign of esteem and confidence!"

"And I was supposed to be grateful for that?" Ninian rasped. "You tossed me a few crumbs from your bounty, and the poor relation was expected to grovel his thanks."

"I never wanted you to grovel," Rupert said quietly. "Man to man, friend to friend, was how I saw it."

"Except that you had everything and I had nothing. I spent my days preserving your estate, making it wealthier . . ."

"I've given you enough money over the years to make you independent. Not just what I paid you, but the money you robbed from me. Oh yes, I know you've been cheating me. I began to suspect recently, and when I studied the books I realized how much you'd stolen. Even then, I forgave you. Your devotion to the estate, to me—the injustice of our relative positions— I made a thousand excuses for you. And then you had Belmont . . ."

"Belmont?" Ninian shrieked, his face distorted. "What was Belmont beside Glennister Court?"

"And for that you became a killer?" Rupert asked in a voice of wonder. "Murder my wife, hang me! I made it easy for you with my reputation, didn't I? The world would have thought me capable of anything. But what can I tell them about you?"

"Do as you please," Ninian snapped. "I'm going to walk out of here. You can call the constable or kill me, or let me go. Make up your mind, and be damned to you!"

He headed for the door. Rupert watched him with alert eyes, but it was Calvina who saw the glint in Ninian's hand.

211

"He's got a gun!" she cried, just as the wicked little weapon was raised swiftly to aim at her.

Rupert moved like lightning, seizing Ninian's arm and trying to wrench the weapon from him. But now Ninian fought back with the ferocity of a man staking all on a final gamble. Calvina held her breath, praying that the gun wouldn't go off and kill Rupert.

Ninian lunged forward one more time. Rupert parried him, thrust him away. Ninian crashed backward, stumbled on a small stool and lost his balance. Too late he saw the open window behind him and flailed frantically. Rupert hurled himself madly across the room, trying to save his cousin, but he was too late. The next moment Ninian had vanished. They heard his scream as he fell four floors, then the sudden silence as he hit the railings.

"Stay back," Rupert said after one glance outside. "It's no sight for you."

"Oh, Rupert!" Calvina wept.

"Hush," he said, taking her into his arms. "It's over. He can hurt us no more. I'll never forgive myself for exposing you to danger, but I trusted him far too long. My darling, my love, say you forgive me."

His lips were on hers in a kiss that told her more truly than words the depth of his love for her. She kissed him back fervently. There were so many things she had to say to him, things which had waited long enough, and still must wait just a little longer.

"Aunt Josie," she said after a while.

"I found her. Sam has carried her to bed and sent for a doctor. I'm afraid there's still much for us to do, this night."

As if in confirmation there was a loud knocking on the street door. "That will be the law," Rupert said. "They've found Ninian."

She clung to him in sudden dread, lest he be blamed for his cousin's death, and torn from her. But the matter passed off far more smoothly than she'd feared. Rupert

212

would have preferred to avoid a scandal by hiding the truth about his cousin, but that wasn't possible. Aunt Josie rose fearlessly from her bed and indignantly told the constable how Ninian had felled her with a blow before trying to kill Calvina. The constable was a middle-aged man who'd once worked for the Glennister family, and he listened sympathetically.

"His fall was an accident," Calvina said. "He thought only of killing us, and he didn't notice the open window. My husband tried to save him, but it was too late."

The constable nodded. "So that's why he was holding a gun when we found him. His finger was still on the trigger. Who'd have thought such a nicely spoken young man would go to the bad? It must be a great sadness to your lordship."

"More sadness than I can say," Rupert replied, with a heaviness in his voice that was entirely genuine.

At last they were all gone, the constable having assured Rupert that he needn't trouble himself about the matter any further. He tried urgently to persuade his aunt to return to bed, but far from being frail, as he'd feared, Josie was alert and determined not to yield to a mere headache, lest she miss anything.

"Then if you're up to the journey," he said, "let us return home. I confess I have a distaste for this place, which will never be overcome. I'll sell it as soon as possible."

The ladies assented eagerly to this plan, and in a few minutes they were in the carriage, heading out of Bath. Aunt Josie dozed. The other two clung tightly, not speaking, but reading the love and truth in each other's eyes. In an hour they were at the Court, where Josie's maid took charge of her and saw her safely to bed.

"I'll get you a hot milk, madam," she suggested.

"Nonsense!" Josie said robustly. "I'll have a large brandy."

When their own bedroom door had closed behind them

213

Lord Rupert seized his wife in a fierce embrace. She went into his arms, raising her face for his kiss, and for a long time they clung together.

"How could you believe I would ever want to harm you?" he said.

"I don't know. It seems so obvious now that it was Ninian, but at the time—he seemed so kind, and I was always a little afraid of you."

"Afraid of that damned foolish reputation of mine. I should have scotched it years ago, but I was too proud. What did the opinions of others matter to me?

"But then there was you, my sweet wife, and it did matter what you thought, although I wouldn't admit it. I'd never met a woman like you, one who could inspire my respect and love as well as desire. You made me want to do whatever would please you, but I didn't know how to. And there was Toby—"

"I never really loved him, Rupert. I realized that long ago."

"You certainly acted like a woman in love. I told myself that I didn't care. And all the time I was too miserable to think straight, and I didn't understand why—until I faced the fact that I was in love with you, that you were the only person who mattered in the world. I kept going away, trying to escape you, but you held my heart, and you always drew me back." He gave a wry grin, directed at himself. "You didn't even know your own power.

"Then I discovered Ninian was cheating me. It burdened my mind, and made me poor company."

"Was that why you've been so grim? I thought it was to do with me."

"Never, never. You've been a joy in my life, and nothing else."

"And—Lysandra?"

"I swear to you that she's nothing to me. She never held my heart, as you do, my dearest. But I thought I owed her something for old times' sake, and I couldn't publicly abandon her when the wolves were closing in. But when we found you gone she had hysterics, and through the wild talk I realized that she'd tried to poison you.

"Suddenly I understood everything. When you'd told me someone was trying to harm you I couldn't bear to believe it was Ninian. But he was the only person who could have given Lysandra that poison, and I saw the truth.

"I went to the General Post Office and found that you'd left on the Bath mail that morning. I drove my curricle like a madman and managed to reach the Court a few minutes before you. I explained everything to Aunt Josie, and she drugged you to get you safely out of the way so that I could deal with Ninian. But he guessed where I'd taken you—"

"Halton was watching," Calvina said. "He's been Ninian's accomplice. It was he on the box of the hack that night."

"Yes, I know. He's been arrested, as well as Lysandra. I meant to keep you safe, but I drove you further into danger. Forgive me, and I'll spend my life making it up to you with my love."

"You truly love me?" she asked breathlessly, almost unable to believe it.

"I think I've loved you from the start. All this time I've longed for you to love me, but I was beginning to lose hope. When you were suspicious of me I was in despair. Tell me that you love me, my darling. For only with your love can I endure life. Without you, the world is nothing."

"You have all my love," she vowed. "It took me too long to understand—but I understand now. I'm yours forever. Let's stay here now, and turn this into a happy home."

"Ah, you can do that. I knew you would change everything the moment we came here." He gave a wry laugh.

215

"Do you remember that strange night? Our wedding night."

"No," she said softly, sliding her arms up around his neck. "This is our wedding night."

Love Letters

Ballantine romances are on the Web!

Read about your favorite Ballantine authors and upcoming books on our Web site, LOVE LETTERS, at **www.randomhouse.com/BB/loveletters**, including:

♥What's new in the stores
♥Previews of upcoming books
♥In-depth interviews with romance authors and
  publishing insiders
♥Sample chapters from new romances
♥And more . . .

Want to keep in touch? To subscribe to Love Notes, the monthly what's-new update for the Love Letters Web site, send an e-mail message to
loveletters@cruises.randomhouse.com
with "subscribe" as the subject of the message. You will receive a monthly announcement of the latest news and features on our site.

So follow your heart and visit us at
www.randomhouse.com/BB/loveletters!